HAIR Very long, very brown, just hanging there like a monumentally bored curtain most days.

EYES Green and framed with glasses you wouldn't even wish on an enemy of the state.

HOME A Victorian house with more books and papers than most libraries.

FAMILY Mum and Dad are university professors, older brother Paul is fun, but more like a family pet than a family member as we just feed and house him and don't expect real human conversation. My best friend Ro is over so often that she's pretty much a part of the family too.

LOVES Books, hanging out in town with Ro and Paul on a 'plenty of people' day, clothes, inventing things, talking too much.

DOES NOT LOVE The way I am a classroom super-brain, but a social super-idiot, my Nick obsession, my glasses, being all dressed up with no place to go but the same place as yesterday and the day before that and the day before that ...

Favourite Website: www.judymaybooks.bebo.com

JUDY MAY grew up in Dublin and is an international traveller and adventurer. She has visited over thirty different countries and has lived in Kathmandu, Paris and New York. She has a degree in Drama and a Masters in literature from Trinity College, Dublin. She used to have a job chaperoning kids and teens on Hollywood film sets, and is proud to be a super-geek! She has also written *Blue Lavender Girl*, *Copper Girl* and *Hazel Wood Girl*.

DIAMOND STAR GIRL

JUDY MAY

THE O'BRIEN PRESS
DUBLIN

First published 2008 by The O'Brien Press Ltd,
12 Terenure Road East, Rathgar, Dublin 6, Ireland.
Tel: +353 1 4923333; Fax: +353 1 4922777
E-mail: books@obrien.ie
Website: www.obrien.ie

ISBN: 978-1-84717-090-3

British Library Cataloguing in Publication Data
A catalogue record for this title is available from the British Library

1 2 3 4 5 6 7 8 9 10
08 09 10 11 12 13 14

The O'Brien Press
receives assistance from

Printed and bound in the UK by J.H. Haynes & Co Ltd, Sparkford

To Uncle Paul, aka Dr Paul Doherty. The best uncle any girl could ever have.

DAY ONE

QUIZ!

If you were almost fifteen, almost a genius, and almost pretty, what would you do with your almost life?

a) Call everyone you know for a fun day of events like boys-against-girls football or a dress-up karaoke party?

b) Start a new action group to combat all crime and poverty on the entire planet?

c) Sit on your ass all afternoon doing a love-compatibility test on the internet?

I tried typing in 'Lemony and Nick,' and it only had a 6 per cent chance of working out. So I put

'Samantha and Nick', and it was 43 per cent, but that wouldn't work either because I would sooner go to town with a pillowcase on my head than have someone call me Samantha again.

According to this precise scientific system, I, Lemony Smith, am perfect for boys called Augustus, Graham and Lucifer (an unbelievable 94 per cent). What's more, I have now wasted five hours of my frankly ridiculous day figuring this out. And it still hasn't stopped me from having eight different, new daydreams about and me and Nick Collins. Things had to stop when I started making him an Olympic marathon champion and dressed him in a sailor uniform to race in. However, I must admit to being rather fond of the one where he rescues me from the freak snowstorm on top of the community hall to where I have escaped following a freak fire caused by a freak misunderstanding with the freaky lady at the homemade-candle stall. The sad fact is that the only freak is me. I know this. I *so* need to get some reality going before I officially turn into a virtual person.

Sometimes I daydream so much I think the house could get swept up in a tornado and I wouldn't even notice. It's like the world inside my head is more real than the one outside, and certainly more interesting.

Maybe writing in this journal will keep me grounded, remind me that there is a world with things and real-live-actual people in it. And boys.

DAY TWO

PROOF OF MY INSANITY: Lorna and Alice asked me to go to this one-day song-writing workshop with their new friend Hanna and I pretended I had to help Mum and Dad with an imaginary leaf problem in the guttering. I do not even know what guttering is and am hoping they don't either. How is anything going to happen if I just stay in with my books and posters creating a big bunch of crazy in my head?

OK, I hereby vow to get OUT of my brain (*brilliant* though it may be) and INTO the world (dull and vacuous as *that* may be). At least the world has one thing going for it: it's where Nick Collins hangs out.

I will now ask Mum and Dad for summer spending money to fund my adventures.

LATER

Yay! Result!

I got twice as much as I bargained for. The money was a 'yes', but now my parents have a new anxiety: that I am unhappy and dissatisfied. In the last ten minutes of the two-hour conversation (for 'conversation' read 'onslaught of friendly-fire and concerned interrogation') they offered to send me on a yoga retreat in India or on a ski-school vacation. I almost said 'yes' to the India thing before Paul piped up with a timely reminder about the last occasion I ate curry. The world may not have done me many favours yet, but it certainly doesn't deserve a repeat of that particular interesting little incident. The ski-school thing will only work when snow stops being cold, and anyway can you ski anywhere in summer?

I love how, as long as I phrase it as a 'learning experience', I can pretty much get anything from Mum and Dad. The girls still can't believe that my kick-ass wardrobe is thanks to an article I mentioned (several times) about a *fascinating* report from MIT and Harvard that I found in one of my recent editions of *Scientific American*. It was about the lifelong damage done to teenage girls when their self-esteem suffers due to lack of ability to fit in clothes-wise (or 'conform sartorially' as the report put it). The folks instantly knew this would mean future therapy bills if I didn't get the skirts, tops, jeans, boots and sneakers I wanted. I guess they did the maths and decided that at least buying me new clothes was a controllable expense; therapy can last forever.

Trouble is, now I just look like a geek in great clothes. It doesn't help that I never know what to do with my hair so it hangs there long and straight, adding to my unkempt-librarian look.

Sadly, the 'academic evidence' thing works both ways with my folks, so I am still not allowed to get contact lenses or get my eyes lasered because of the medical write-ups that my darling brother put under their noses about dry-eye syndrome and infections leading to blindness. What super-bites is that the main article came from one of my own copies of *Time* magazine. In all honesty, having eyes like shrivelled raisins or dripping with gungy bits would be heaven compared to wearing old-lady glasses with frames thick enough to fit french doors into. I chose them last year thinking that if I went for the geekiest, ugliest, frumpiest pair, they'd look ironic, the way rock stars sometimes carry it off, but sadly they just look geeky, ugly and wronger than wrongness itself.

I'm just ranting now.

I should use this journal to plan exact things and carry them out and report back. Righty-ho! Task number one in the Reality Game – go into town and talk to five new teenagers from the regulars who hang out there, but who I don't know properly. These will be five who do *not* either a) say that they *have* to get out of this town or they will go mad or b) look like they might have rickets or scurvy or too much pink stuff in their wardrobe (especially true of males).

Good luck, Lemony, and Godspeed!

STILL LATER

OK, *not* so easy. It gets to that moment where there's someone new and roughly your age looking at you, and you are smiling at them trying not to look like you just had dental work done. But then what do you do next? With one girl I muttered 'nice bag' and she muttered 'thanks', and that was it. I mean, what could I do after that, say, 'nice jacket' or something?

I'd have sounded like a simpleton. And as for guys, if you even hold eye contact for too long you feel like a stalker. And if you say anything nice then they say something sly about you to their friends and suddenly you have become their afternoon's entertainment. And I have heard every comment there is about 'four-eyes', and 'what's the weather like up there?' and I need to protect myself from that.

And then there was Nick hanging out by the fountain, looking like God himself, and all he did was say, 'Where's your twin?' (meaning Ro, of course). I can't believe he hasn't got tired of saying that and *still* hasn't bothered remembering our names. I think he thinks it's hilarious because although we do spend a ridiculous amount of time together, with my height and her lack of it, and my boring, long, brown hair and her stunning, black dreads, we are about as twin-like as a giraffe and a grizzly bear. I am now convinced that the love-test thing with the names is wrong (scientifically as well as morally) because it's feeling like my odds with the Nick-man are sitting *way* below 6 per cent.

I wonder what else they eat in India?

I just love him *so* much that it hurts. What also hurts is when people presume that because I'm so cheery and brainy that I simply don't care about stuff like that. Not that I cry much. I wonder why I do that, just stuff it down inside and put a smile on my face and think of something witty to say. I think that if I cried then I would feel worse and somehow they would have made me less.

Why does he only go for the stunningly glamorous girls? Has he got something against personality and brains? Really and truly, does a girl have to be a celebrity or get crowned Miss Northern Hemisphere to get a bit of attention round here?

I think the group from town would be amazed if they knew how often I get dressed to go out to a party or dance and then sit on the edge of my bed, too scared in case I'm all wrong. That's why they think I prefer doing schoolwork and science projects to hanging out. Nothing could be less true (except maybe the 6 per cent thing).

One very cool aspect to this summer is that there is no science camp this year because they blew up one of the labs with an acid/alkali experiment that they'd been planning for the eight-year-olds to do. And seeing as my suggestion of going to a modelling and deportment seminar was laughed out of the inner atmosphere by my loving family, I need to make my own fun this summer. They think they know me so well, my family, but how do they know for definite that I'll never need to get out of a sports car without flashing my underwear, or need to know how to apply mascara in seven thin coats? It might just save us all one day! I think Paul should go to it so at least he'll stop snorting milk out of his nose when he laughs at me.

This is the problem with being an imaginative trail-blazer, a self-improver: by the time anyone gets your brilliance you've already moved on to greater greatnesses.

My brilliance? Yeah, right, I guess I must be thinking about those health-shoes I designed and made with the ventilation holes that also let rain in, or the spy-boots with the secret compartment in the right heel that made me walk with a limp, or the time I made my own board game called 'Mess', like chess, but with more pieces and fewer rules. At this point Paul would say it's no wonder I don't have more friends and Ro would hit him.

Face it. I am nothing but a bundle of potential with a large vocabulary and larger glasses.

DAY THREE

Emergency! Is there a social worker in the house?

Mum and Dad are having another of their University Professors' gatherings, where they scrape together all *the* most boring, dusty people on campus and ask them to bring along their kids to torture me and Paul further. *I* do not deserve torture so they should let me be anywhere else on the planet that night and leave Paul to drown in talk about grants, publications and advanced placements.

They broke the news to us over breakfast and told us that we had to wear our nice clothes (*their* version of nice), and that we would have to prepare finger food *and* interesting bits of 'cocktail conversation'.

Paul put on his fake-serious face and said,

'Mum, Dad, what have we EVER done to you?'

But then Dad had a list for that one ready in his head.

I asked Ro about what I could use for cocktail conversation and she said that when her mother has a cocktail or two she starts to talk about her cellulite and how she missed the opportunity to be a backing singer for a man who once made it to number 23 in the charts because of her own mother's triple-bypass. Not sure if that's what the folks have in mind, but I'm now tempted to sneak Ro's mum in through the back door on the night.

As usual, instead of having a direct and civilised conversation about the things that are bothering them, the folks are worrying about me in a sideways fashion. Dad has been asking me how my 'premature midlife crisis' is coming along and Mum put this old book on my bed from the 1920s, called *The Game Of Life And How To Play It* by Florence Scovel-Shinn. I could just tell them that I'm fine, but on a practical note I might soon need more money! No really, I like it when they check up on me; it makes a change from the way they disappear into piles of research papers and dissertations for days on end.

I just finished the book and it's all about how if you expect great things to happen and visualise and 'speak the word' then the universe will deliver you what you want. Sort of like casting spells or making wishes, or like a cool, scientific experiment! According to the book, the human mind can affect things at a subatomic level just by thinking or looking at a particle. Anyway, this book is much lighter than any of the popular science books I've read before now, not 'lab-based' at all. There's a story in it about throwing your lucky monkeys down a coal hole, which I didn't really get (probably because I have neither). But there was a cool one about this lady who had almost no money who went out and bought a really expensive lunch and because she did it (showing she knew that riches were on the way) then big money arrived just in time. Interesting! Maybe I'll do some more research and see if any modern studies have been done on this ...

If the book is right, then I've been confusing the universe *so* much – first wanting Nick to rescue me from a roof, then from a burning bus shelter, then wanting him to be a prince in a small European state ... that the universe has given up on me entirely!

All I need to do is learn how to hold one idea steadily enough for it to come about. If this stuff actually works then I need never feel frustrated again.

OK, now for the real science bit – I need to set up a way of finding out if it's true, if all you have to do is say those phrases and conjure up the right pictures to make stuff happen the way you want it to.

From now on I will imagine myself as a movie star and say 'Thank you for making me a movie star'. Not that I actually want to *be* one, it's just that it would be a good, clear test for this subject and heaven knows I need the attention. If it works I can then ditch the whole film star gig, start using my new-found powers for more important stuff like going out with Nick, and getting a chinchilla for my birthday. It is the only thing close to daydreaming that I am going to allow, that way I won't be sending out muddy orders and getting muddy results.

LATER

Ro came over and liked the book too (it doesn't take long to read). She has decided to focus on selling one of her paintings in a big art gallery. I told her to make it a larger, tougher goal as her art is already amazing and she is so good at getting things done that it wouldn't test the theory of the thing, but she was adamant. We decided not to include Paul on this one because he'd only choose something disgusting to gross us out like making all the flesh fall away from his right forearm without touching it, or becoming best friends with a tarantula trainer.

Granted, magic circles are a bit like something we used to do back when we played with Barbies, but we made a space with scarves and in the middle lit a cinnamon candle, which must have been left over from Christmas. Next we put tokens of our goals into a small box – a tube of paint for Ro and a photo of me with a tiara and false eye-lashes from Lorna's last pj-party along with some little gold confetti stars. While I was in the kitchen fetching matches and a timer I found this meditation music that Mum did Pilates exercises to that one single time (having bought the mat, the scary leotard and the whole set of music).

Ro locked the door while I drew the curtains, then we put on the music, closed our eyes and spent ten minutes imagining ourselves with the dreams-come-true in progress. I saw myself under bright lights with a make-up girl fussing over me, and then I was checking over my lines in a script. Then just as I was walking over to the crowd to sign autographs the kitchen timer buzzed so loudly that I knocked over the candle and wax went everywhere. Ro thinks this is a good omen. I think it is a good sign that we are both bored beyond belief.

I thanked Mum for the book at dinner and Dad and Paul were too afraid to ask, 'What book?' in case it was some girl thing.

DAY FOUR

I am now officially not speaking to anyone. The only problem is that no one has tried to speak to *me* so I haven't been able to alert them to this turn of affairs.

The Story Of Lemony Smith's Heartbreaking Humiliation and Social Downfall (not that there was all that far to fall in the first place).

I was in town with Mum because she is all excited about the party and felt a burning need to buy me the kind of outfit I wouldn't even let myself be buried in (though I suppose it doesn't matter what I wear for a house full of people who think Einstein had a 'fun' haircut). But that's not the bad bit. The true horror started as we walked from the shoe shop on the corner (the big one, not the one that Ro likes) to the car park, and out of the habit of centuries she grabbed my hand to cross the road. Suddenly, there was pretty much *everyone* I know and who I care about whether they like me, sitting on the wall. *All* the cool people just sitting there like a Saturday morning wall club or something. It was as if they lined up there on purpose to both cause *and* witness my social destruction. ABSOLUTE NIGHTMARE. Nick, Suzette, Fintan, Hanna, Saul, Johnny L, Marty, Gussy, Amber, Jonty, Lara, Kristin, Dave, Alice, Bonnie, Dairne, Mark, Ed ... all of them. And Nick, did I mention that Nick Collins was there? Of course if I'd have dressed up and gone into town with hope of finding them they'd have all stayed at home. And it's not like they were mean or anything, they just sort of looked at me walking past with my mum and none of us said 'hello', in fact none of us said anything. That was so *weird* because we are always really loud with our 'hellos' and hugs even if we run out of stuff to say after that. I was *dying*. I can't face any of them again. The worst part, and I don't even want to write it down, was that I was carrying Mum's huge plastic tartan bag, the really old one that you wouldn't even house a stray puppy in. I will now never, ever have a social life, not even if I apply to Amnesty International. Even years from now the whole gang of them will be like,

'Oh yeah, Lemony Smith, the one that got a Golden Globe and an Oscar. Did you know her mum still picked out her clothes when she was a teenager? Good thing she has a team of stylists now, not a shiny tartan grocery bag in sight!'

And then they will get back to inviting each other round for barbecues without me.

It was just the most evil moment of my life and there isn't even anyone to blame. Even though it is not yet lunchtime I am now going back to bed. Forever. And I am not speaking to anyone.

LATER

I am now speaking to Ro, Paul and the folks, and that's all.

Ro brought around a clipping from the local paper about acting classes so I had to explain to her that I don't actually *want* to be an actress, it's just that being a film star is as far from being me as I could imagine, so it made for a great way of testing the idea that you can make things happen by using the power of your mind. It's a life-as-laboratory kind of thing.

I told her about the wall fiasco and she says that the others probably thought that maybe I didn't want my mum to know that I'm friends with them, what with some of them looking so close-to-the-edge with the piercings and hair. I still believe it is more likely that *they* don't want to know *me* since finding out that I go shopping with my mum (who just HAD to be talking about lost underwear in the laundry room at the time) and that I am capable of carrying such unfortunate objects as the grocery bag. If Bonnie, Dairne or Amber ever even *saw* a shopping bag it would be Gucci or Prada. I'm not ashamed of Mum or anything, it's just that I already have to work hard to get anyone's approval that I don't have any coolness credit in the bank when something like this happens.

Ro is so much more of an insider socially. I don't know how she manages to do that and still spend so much time with me. Everyone knows and loves her. She looks like the cutest little pixie you ever saw, with her dark green eyes, tiny frame and black hair in dreads to her shoulders, all the guys fancy her and the girls admire her. I've never felt jealous, but I do wish I had some more of that magic myself.

'Ro' is short for 'Aphrodite'. She's been called 'Ro'

for as long as I've known her. When we were tiny I really wanted to have a cute nickname like hers – everyone called me 'Sam' back then, which was the same name as one of Ro's dogs! It was Paul who started calling me 'Lemony'; I ran into the kitchen one day when I was about five wearing a yellow t-shirt and he said,

'You look like a lemon! Yeah, lemon-y, definitely.'

It became sort of a nickname that stuck. Of course a few months later the first in a series of books came out, written by someone with the same first name! But no one mentioned it, so I guess they just associated Lemony with me by that stage.

Then Paul decided he wanted to be called Charles for about a week, but that changed when Dad began to yell up the stairs, 'Is Bonny Prince Charlie in?' whenever someone called.

I know it's weird to hang out with your brother, but he's only a year older than me and he's really hilarious to be around. Most importantly, he doesn't think that me and Ro are annoying just because we're younger. He thinks we are annoying for a whole bunch of other reasons.

Ro locked my bedroom door and we did the visualising and declaring for our wishes again this evening, and this time I put Nick in as the leading man. I thought, 'What's the harm?' Have to be a professional about it after all.

Still *dying* about the other thing.

DAY FIVE

Avoiding cake and chocolate may be less than easy, but it's almost *impossible* not to daydream. It may not be my intention to get lost in Nick-and-Lemony's loveland, but I know it must be happening because it doesn't take anyone forty minutes to brush their teeth. Either I was daydreaming for a large chunk of that time or I have been blessed with the gums of a rhino.

The parent party looms. Luckily Paul warned me that they had a plan for us that involved washing and ironing tablecloths and suchlike so we crept out early this morning and switched off our phones. Once we got to the café Paul was too busy entertaining his fan club of older waitresses, so I didn't get to share the whole wall-bag-silence disaster with him as I'd planned. And the chance never came because just as I cleared the layer of foam from my hot chocolate, in walked half the regiment from yesterday's little stand-off.

The evidence is in, the votes have been counted and there is no denying, I am REALLY bad at not speaking to people. The moment Nick, Hanna, Alice, Dairne, Jonty and Gussy walked over to where Paul and I were sitting, my mouth kicked into action and didn't stop until it had said ten times more than the moment required.

I do believe my actual words were,

'Oh hi, ... hi, .. yeah, ... sorry about yesterday, you know, ... with my mum, ... you know, shopping, well of course, ... good to see you, ... funny, wasn't it? ... or not, maybe, well, ... how are you?'

And thank goodness Hanna cut in and went,

'Great, all doing great, thanks Lem,' because she fancies Paul on-and-off and wants to look all kind and uncomplicated in front of him.

Just when I thought that it was all over, that the ice had been broken and the incident might be put behind us, Nick goes,

'So where's your shopping bag, taller twin?'

Gussy laughed, but that's OK because he suffers badly from idiot syndrome and everyone knows it. But why did Nick have to do that to me???

Alice was lovely and while the others ordered drinks she whispered that they all thought I wouldn't want them saying 'Hi' in front of my mum, and that some of them felt bad about it after I left. Later she told me that they all talked about how funny and intelligent I am, which made me feel worse because it was really them NOT saying that I was pretty or cool or anything. Also Alice is really sweet and always wanting people to feel good so sometimes it's hard to tell how much she is exaggerating the good stuff.

I hung around a bit more before guilt kicked in at the thought of Mum and Dad doing all the work themselves. Paul keeps his guilt in a much smaller box and stayed while I headed home (as soon as Nick left, of course) to take over the chopping board and cut the crusts off ten loaves of bread.

I hoped I might pass someone good on the way back, but I only saw that awful Stephen Brown who used to be in Paul's class and now goes to an international boarding school. We used to call him

'Brown Stephen' because he always wore brown jumpers and trousers and tortoiseshell glasses. I guess if he's home from school he'll be at the party with his dad tonight ... just when you thought it was safe to go back in the water of life.

Having spent the last six hours polishing already perfectly shiny bits of furniture and silverware I am now pretending to take ages to get ready, even though less than four minutes will do the job.

I can hear people being relieved of their coats. Within five minutes I will be listening to people say how much I've grown and how they'd better stop feeding me string beans. Must remember that all the great people of history had to have miserable beginnings in order to make the 'hero bit' look and feel good.

Right, time to get courageous and pitch in for the glory of the Smith family armed with only a fixed grin and a tray of sad-looking hors d'oeuvres.

DAY SIX

OK, it is now late morning and the best thing I can say is that everyone survived, even most of the sandwiches survived and are alive and well and stocking up the fridge for us to eat over the course of the next millennium. I think Mum got overly confident about the ability of ham and fennel to mix, and the ability of people to eat more than ten mini scotch-eggs each after sundown. Pear and anchovy was another bold move on her part.

The worst thing is that Stephen Brown was there as predicted and he is a *proper* geek whereas I am an undercover goddess of wit and sophistication *masquerading* as a geek for the time being. Heavily masquerading, granted. You could tell that he was loving it, probably the only time he's been out since he was here four years ago. And this isn't one of those things where a boy you knew when you were younger was annoying and then he is all transformed and magnificent when you meet him in your teens. Although he no longer dresses exclusively in brown, and seems to have lost his glasses, he still looks as if nothing quite fits. And if there was a Nobel prize on offer for being inane and conceited he'd be well famous by now. *And* it's not going to be one of those Mr Darcy things where I turn out to be wrong about him and he was actually lovely all the time. Honestly, the guy is INFURIATING, the way he picked all the onions from the quiche before eating it, and the way he laughed at what my mother was saying even though I know for a FACT that she has never been funny even once in the last fourteen years. I mean she is an absolute *darling,* just not funny. Luckily he is my brother's age and for some strange reason Paul wasn't as allergic to him as I was.

Oh, *AND* of course geek-boy is very tall and speaks fluent Chinese, which for some reason made all the adults assume I would be fascinated by him. I mean, he didn't even have to learn it because he lived in Shanghai until he was six, so it's not like its a *real* accomplishment, but he grinned so much whenever his dad mentioned it that you can tell he thinks it makes him amazing. Which it *doesn't*. I mean, if the leftover sandwiches could speak Chinese that wouldn't be enough to make *them* palatable either. I am off to buy scones.

DAY SEVEN

Sorry, sorry, I take it all back! My life is incredible! Nick called to the door at ten in the morning, and luckily I had just spent half an hour getting ready to go into town. So I took my boots off before walking downstairs so that he would think that I normally look this good for hanging round the house. Anyway, he asked me to go to the junior musical-and-dramatic society dance with him next week. I don't need to be a film star after all, I've got what I really wanted all along.

I now have to go and spend twenty hours talking this over with Ro.

LATER

I'm glad the whole Nick asking me out thing happened this morning so I was in good enough shape to hear the news from Mum about having to repeat last night's torture in a whole new venue. Tomorrow night we are being made to go to Professor Brown's house, The Grange, for dinner. What is it with these college lecturers and their need to congregate over bad cooking and talk about things that have been dead for centuries? Worse still, Paul is excused because of cricket practice. I begged them to let me take up cricket, but by 6pm tomorrow I am doomed to being more bored and starving than a supermodel. I hope Dad was joking when he recommended I brush up on my Chinese.

I have taken everything out of my wardrobe and will spend the rest of the evening practising looking casually and effortlessly fantastic in several different outfits for the dance. The girls are coming over in the morning to help with the final decision.

In three days I will be Nick's girlfriend and all will be right with the world.

DAY EIGHT

It hurts, it hurts, it hurts. I can't believe it, just when I thought that maybe I wasn't a complete social stain and he goes and ruins it all on me, telling me he has a new girlfriend. AND he said it as if still going to the dance, but 'as friends' was good idea!!!!! I don't even hate her for it, or him, I just hate me right now. I asked him why he'd asked me in the first place and he said it was because it would be obvious that we were going 'as friends' and there would have been no pressure. So he never thought of it as a date in the first place AND he thinks that going out with me would be something no one would ever believe!!

And Paul was *no* help whatsoever, talking as if

Nick was a massive hero for being honest about the whole thing. I mean, if he'd gone and stuck his head in a moving sawmill, THAT might have been the kind of heroic gesture I could celebrate. Being honest?! An honest-to-God MISTAKE OF A PERSON!

Ro and Lorna came over to tell me the news and Nick himself phoned an hour later. They left Alice behind because she was actually in tears about it and it wasn't even about her. Apparently a few of them were at Johnny L's house and somehow Nick and Donna ended up on the patio kissing. He told her that he was going to the dance with me, but 'as friends', which she then told Amber so now half the country knows.

If Paul says, 'But he wasn't officially your boyfriend', one more time I swear I will do something unnatural. *How* can that be helpful? It's like saying to someone whose rented house burned down,

'But it wasn't yours and you were only living there for two years.'

Two years is how long I waited for him to ask me out. Two years! Most Hollywood marriages don't last that long and Paul thinks I can shake it off just because Nick never kissed me or gave me his leather bomber-jacket to wear or whatever. I want to do *something, anything* to make Nick sorry, but I know I'll just act really pally with him and Donna next time to make people think I was never into him in that way.

I cried a bit and then stopped and paced around, and then started joking about hoping Nick was still going to pay me for agreeing to go to the dance with him in the first place. So Lorna thinks I'm over it, but Ro knows me better than that. Tough girls like Lorna and really soft girls like Alice have it easier when it comes to making a fuss. I wish I could shout or cry or anything to get the bad feeling out of me. But instead I am choosing the journal-as-therapy route.

Even during writing this I have checked my messages so often my thumb is sore from pressing the keys. As if he might be trying desperately to contact me and tell me he has made the biggest mistake of his life and it's made him see that it's really me he wants after all.

And I still have to go to the stupid dinner at The Grange in two hours time.

DAY NINE

I have decided to have the mumps. Not for real of course, but for the purposes of getting out of being Nick's friend for the evening of the dance while he makes eyes at Donna who will no doubt be busy being all mature about the situation across the room.

I called Ro and Paul into my room for an intervention.

'Why can't he get himself sorted and like me?' I wailed.

Paul said something about Nick liking me just not in *that* way, which was *so* uncalled for and outrageously too much truth given the situation.

Good thing Ro always has a practical-sounding answer that makes me feel good. She is the most practical person I know, she even has her own screwdriver set and emergency cash, which she doesn't spend on shoe emergencies the way I would. Very weird for someone so fashionable and cute not to be in the least bit flaky. She doesn't even get crazy over guys, she just sees one she likes, dates him them dumps him when she feels she's outgrown him (usually after three weeks or so).

Anyway, when I asked why Nick isn't into me, she said,

'It's because he's a guy and they are always at least five years behind where they should be. My mum said that Dad is now exactly the man she wanted half a decade ago.'

'You could be right,' I sighed, 'I mean Paul here only stopped wetting the bed last week! Hey! You're not allowed punch me when I'm depressed! Hit Ro instead, it's her theory.'

'Three years from now Nick Collins will be kicking himself,' Ro continued. 'And where will you be, Lemony my girl? Off in a private jet with some guy who doesn't fancy Donna.'

'Or I'll be here, with you and Paul and a new

cinnamon candle and the same problems,' I said.

'No, Lem. You'll have *much* better problems by then,' Ro smiled.

'We'll make sure of that,' Paul added helpfully.

Somehow I didn't feel that much better. It seems that ever since the summer holidays began I'm either having a bad day or recovering from one.

'When does it all get good?' I wondered.

'Soon, funny girl, very soon,' Ro reassured me.

'And when do I get to be one of the beautiful ones?'

'That happens, dear sister, as soon as you can afford the surgery.'

And with that Ro ordered Paul out of the room. She is the only person who can control him. I think this is because she has three dogs and there are training similarities.

Oh, and the dinner last night was fine. It was made easier by the fact that The Grange is *such* a cool place, and they have a caterer or cook to do the food *and* Stephen has a friend called Alex staying with him who is very easy on the eye and doesn't speak a word of Chinese. Alex's dad is a film producer and is shooting a film in town so he'll be here for the summer. He's not the kind of guy for me as he has really dark spiky hair and he's at least five inches shorter than me, I know that shouldn't matter, but it docs to me so there you go. After dinner Stephen, Alex and I went off to the upstairs library while our parents good-naturedly debated something that you need to be fluent in dull to understand.

I admit to being a complete sucker for a house-library and this is the best I've ever seen. It has floor to ceiling mahogany shelves and huge leaded windows, and the books are all over a hundred years old, leather-bound with gilt lettering. It had grown a bit chilly so their housekeeper lit a turf fire in the fireplace, and we sank into these huge leather armchairs. Alex told us about a film he worked on last summer as an extra, while Stephen and I listened, which I think suited all of us just fine. I hope Stephen doesn't think we're friends because of being in his company twice in one week. Imagine if he came up to me when I was with the others in town and presumed he could hang out. I don't want to be mean, but I'm close enough to being an outcast as it is, and a geek like him would hardly make anyone look like a social superstar.

By now all anger over Nick has morphed into complete humiliation and I am hoping that by tomorrow it will have faded to a slight shame. And *that* I can live with because I know it so well. I'd love a life free of feeling like the freak of the universe.

Ro wanted to do the manifesting circle thing again tonight to imagine being a film star and famous artist, but I didn't have the heart for it. What's the point of being a film star if the guy you fancy is going out with Donna Henderson?

She also said that flu would be better than mumps so I can recover in time to be back in town looking stunning the day after. Of course she is right.

DAY TEN

In the end I gave myself a better offer instead of an infectious disease and contacted Nick with the news that I'd been invited to dinner with an important family friend and wouldn't be able to go to the dance.

Mum needed help with tidying away all the things we took out of storage for the party so that has taken up most of today. It's now early in the evening so I think I might try that visualising and speaking the word about being an actress, just because it hurts too much to think about Nick and he keeps creeping back into my head. At least this way if he does sneak back in he'll have competition from hunky leading men.

I have written it out on a piece of paper, everything that I intend to have happen, and Ro has done the same over at her place and we're going to hang onto them until we can organise to float them out to sea or burn them in a ceremonial … er … ceremony I guess.

Mine is written in the dark purple ink I use for journalling, and it fills a page that I ripped from the back of this. It says:

WHEN THESE THINGS HAPPEN MY LIFE IS PERFECT

I am a proper film star.

I am Nick Collins' official girlfriend.

Mum has stopped asking me would I not like to do something with my hair.

Dad has let me take up the saxophone and has agreed that Chinchillas are the easiest pets to keep.

Boring Brown Stephen stays as far away as possible and stops kidding himself that we are friends.

LATER

I was doing all this meditating, laundry, reading difficult books and clearing out of cupboards, checking out stuff on the computer in the sitting room (one computer and fifty million books – what a house!) and just about anything to get my mind off the fact that I was NOT snogging Nick behind the stage at the junior M&D dance, when the freakiest thing happened! This could make the summer interesting after all and not the marshland of self-pity it was panning out to be. This very minute I've just returned from meeting with the girls and it's still sinking in. You'd think I'd be used to surprises by now, taking into account all the practice I've been given this week.

HERE IT IS!

Boring Brown Stephen phoned (must start calling him Stephen in case that slips out some time) and Mum refused to pretend I wasn't in like I asked her to. I was *praying* he wasn't going to ask me on a date or anything, but in fact his dad made him phone me, a point which was made *very* clear in the first minute of the conversation. He explained that Alex's dad, the film producer, has arranged to shoot part of his movie at The Grange, because it's a historical drama and they need a huge old house with grounds. AND film-producer-dad wanted Alex and Stephen to find teenagers to audition for sixteen teen extra parts in the film, eight guys and eight girls. At first I thought he wanted me to introduce him to some teenagers who might be good, but in fact he wants ME to audition too! I so heavily hinted about how perfect Ro and the others would be that by the end of the conversation he asked would I mind choosing loads of other girls to audition because he doesn't know any in town anymore apart from me. The job of an extra is pretty easy from what Alex told us the other night, you're just in a costume in the background pretending to speak and eat or whatever is going on in the scene.

Stephen said to gather up as many girls as possible and be in his house tomorrow after lunch to meet the assistant director who will make the final decision. I then passed him over to Paul who he asked to audition too and bring loads of guys (Alex and Stephen have already been cast as extras, nepotism rules!).

I chose Ro, Lorna and Alice, Hanna, Dairne, Amber and Bonnie. My thinking was that if there are only just enough of us, then we'll all get chosen. Mum made me invite my cousin Sophie even though she is only twelve and we have enough girls already. I'm now scared that they won't choose me because there will be one too many and I'm too tall. If that happens I will never forgive Mum, but she's talking about it like it's a kid's birthday party and everyone's invited.

I keep going from thrilled to annoyed and back again in the space of two seconds.

Even though it was late, within an hour all us girls met in Hanna's den, which is cool, with computers and music systems and speakers all over the place, and three huge couches that she and her brothers liberated from skips in the middle of the night.

We have decided that when we go there we're not going to dress up too much, we're just going to wear what we would normally wear on a Saturday in town, jeans and that, and to take it easy on the make-up. We'll meet back at Hanna's for a pasta lunch tomorrow and then all go straight to Professor Brown's house from there.

DAY ELEVEN

It was hilarious. We all showed up in our best party outfits and wearing *way* more make-up than usual and enough accessories to stock a medium-sized department store.

It didn't matter anyway because when we got there and our pictures were taken they were barely glanced at by the Assistant Director, Lizzy (she's called the Third AD as apparently there are two others more senior to her). She told us that we were all hired! Alex later explained that casting extras on a movie isn't a big deal and as long as you don't have a third arm or a terribly obvious hump then you're in. It still felt great to be chosen though.

The only bad bit was that it's a historical costume drama and Hanna would have to get the blue-black dye taken out of her hair and lose the goth make-up (which she's cool with) and Ro was told that she'd need to un-dread her hair. She said she would never do that and would prefer not to be involved in the film at all. I was totally panicking about her not being in it with me when Lizzy, I think seeing Ro's eyes well up with tears (as well as Alice's of course!), said that there was a job going as assistant to the location manager and would Ro like to talk to him about it.

So Ro went off with Lizzy to meet the location manager while the rest of us went home. Dairne can't do it as she's going on holiday halfway through, but she doesn't seem to mind.

I am SO excited! I know it's about as far from being a film star as a burger-flipper is from being a Michelin-star chef, but at least we'll be busy for the next month and they'll be paying us so I won't need to bug Mum and Dad for money any more.

Lizzy is meeting the guys tomorrow so I'm off to ask Paul who's auditioning.

LATER

I nearly fell off my feet when Paul told me that he asked Nick to audition. I yelled at him for a good two minutes until I had to breathe and he smartly pointed out that if Nick and I are working on set, and Donna isn't, then it's the perfect situation. I had to admit he had a point, and then I had to go and calm myself down with several cups of tea. It's all very trying this love business. He'll get chosen for sure as Paul only bothered to ask five guys.

The book *The Game Of Life*, talks about acting on hunches, and I have a weird feeling that I am supposed to go talk to Lorna and Alice, although I only saw them two hours ago and we've said all there is to say and then some.

DAY TWELVE

The hunch about calling around to Lorna's last night was a good one. I found her stomping around like a woodsman, with Alice crouched in a ball on a chair all pale and puffy-faced from crying even more than usual. Apparently their parents phoned each other and agreed that show business was not an inspirational or nurturing environment for young women, and they are not allowed to even the *visit* the set, let alone work there! Alice's father believes that she'll be running off to Hollywood and destroying her chances of becoming a quantum physicist. He must be the only person on the planet who doesn't know that when she's older she wants to make hats.

I managed to calm down the hysterics, and get them in a state where they could start to find solutions. I handled Lorna by telling her that stomping is a sign of weakness, and Alice by giving her my back-up bar of chocolate. Both agreed to persuade their parents to come over to my house this afternoon.

Once I got back I explained the whole scenario to Dad who phoned Professor Brown to come over today to meet Alice and Lorna's parents. Luckily they all know each other because Alice's mum lectures in the maths department and Lorna's parents are both head librarians. I asked Dad would he rather I was hanging out with girls we've known since I was born, or unknown new girls who might be into weirdness. I believe he's now putting on his fix-it cap.

LATER

Even better than I imagined! Not only are they allowed to be in the film, but the whole group of us, well half of us anyway, are going to stay at The Grange during filming. Me, Ro, Paul, Alice (who has decided not to throw herself from the top of the bell tower after all), and Lorna (who is no longer looking at serving life in prison for killing someone with a hard stare). The parental logic (ha!) is that we can get in less trouble if we are all under one roof where Professor Brown can keep an eye on us. I have no clue why they think that might mean *less* trouble, but I'm certainly not going to argue against it. Also it solves the problem of how to get us all to the set on time every day. The downer is that the teen extras who live on the other side of town (including Nick) won't be staying at The Grange due to lack of room and the fact that there is a bus that will be picking them up and dropping them back. They all live within a couple of streets of each other so I guess it makes sense.

It feels weird packing a suitcase to go fifteen minutes up the road. At least I can leave all my books behind because the library at The Grange has enough to last even me for a lifetime. I'm sort of glad that so much less happens during the school year, I'd be a wreck if life always barrelled along at this speed.

Right, as soon as Ro gets here we're off.

I'm writing this from my cushioned nook on a wide window-sill in the library room at The Grange. The equipment trucks, actors and crew don't arrive until the day after tomorrow so we have a little time to settle in. The Professor asked us to come a couple of days early to get accustomed to the place, but I suspect he's just desperate to provide more company for his awkward son. Also Mum and Dad are preparing for a huge symposium they'll be off to in a couple of weeks so it suited them to have us out of the way.

This morning I was up first, and was showered, dressed and out walking the grounds before the others were awake. For an hour I simply wandered up and down the paths and around the orchard and the greenhouse, sitting on a bench every now and then to listen to the birds. God, I hope no one finds this, they will think I am soft in the head. Actually, they'll already think I'm weird if they've read this far, the hanging out on a bench like a spare old-person will only confirm it.

Breakfast was in the formal dining room, a buffet of pancakes, toast, cereal, eggs, kippers (really!), juice, tea, muffins, bagels, and fruit salad. It was strange how we all sat up straighter than usual and watched our language even though there was only the eight of us and no adults around. There is a lovely lady called Miss Higgins who waddled and pottered in and out who wouldn't even let us help clear away the dishes or stack the dishwasher. Could get used to this. Paul already is.

It reminded me of an old-fashioned boarding-school novel when we arrived last night. The four of us girls – me, Ro, Lorna and Alice – are in one of the two large attic rooms with a double bed each, two large old wardrobes, and a small chest of drawers beside each bed. There's a gorgeous new soft carpet on the floor that smells the way only new carpets can, and fresh nets and cream curtains on the windows.

Stephen has moved out of his usual bedroom and into the other attic room with Alex, Paul and Gussy (just my luck!). Apparently the other ten bedrooms (apart from the Professor's room) are being used as extras' dressing rooms, production HQ, wardrobe department storage rooms and a props room. Most of our news is filtering in through Ro who pops into the house every couple of hours with lists and speaking into a walkie talkie. It is so completely Ro to look as if she's been doing it for years, she's a natural at organising, and not just dogs and other people's brothers. Bob, the location manager put her onto the job as soon as they met and she's an old pro already.

It's their job to make sure that the location where the filming happens has everything they will need, water, power and all that, that people and trucks can get in and out, and that nothing gets damaged. Only two days in and she's taking photos of walls and stairs, ordering gardeners to move urns and garden furniture and saying things like, 'Roger that Bob!' and, 'Bob, the access gate is four point eight metres wide, but there is the possibility of removing the gates to gain an extra point five. Let me know.'

I am so proud of my little dungareed friend.

Stephen (who actually dresses pretty normal these days in jeans and t-shirts) gave us a tour of the place. It's all fairly straightforward (if huge); two kitchens, two pantries, a utility room and storage rooms in the basement, a huge entrance hall on the ground floor with two sitting rooms to either side in the front, and a larger reception room behind with a ballroom on one side and an impossibly large dining room on the other. The library, the billiards room and the Professor's office are on a kind of return up a short staircase at the back of the house, looking out onto the cobbled courtyard.

Then up the central staircase are ten bedrooms, five to each side along the two corridors and an en-suite bathroom off each room, which were put in a few years ago. The whole house smells of wood, furniture-polish and old books, and makes me feel like I'm back living three centuries ago. I wonder if Stephen knows how lucky he is to be brought up here. He was showing off the portraits of his ancestors to Alice when I slipped away to come here.

The best of all (apart from the library) is our part of the house. You have to go up these long, rickety side stairs and then stoop as you go into the landing where our two attic dorms look out onto the main garden. The grounds extend just as far as you can see, so they are huge, but not like a park or wilderness. Thank God there is a bathroom for each of us across the landing, the thought of sharing a toilet with Gussy would be enough to send me home.

Paul confirmed my prediction that Alex would have more toiletries and products than all the girls put together. Alex is cool, although there's not much going on in his head except for names of people I'm apparently supposed to know from movies. He definitely has a thing for Lorna, but she's never in her life had time for his brand of nonsense, so all his singing of Frank Sinatra and Dean Martin to her is falling on eaf ears. They look quite alike, loads of teeth, dark hair and dark eyes, not that you should choose each other based on that. Anyway she'd eat him alive, so I guess I admire his courage.

LATER

So much for Professor Brown keeping an eye on us, we've just had a rock-out party in one of the kitchens. It's amazing how much fun you can have with a batch of bruschettas, a case of bottled juices and a bunch of people who can't sing nearly as well as they think they can. It was the BEST, especially when Ro and Lorna were dancing on a table while Paul and Alex sang some seriously dodgy song that none of us have ever heard, but they insist is a classic.

Stephen doesn't think much of me either which is a relief as it means I don't have to push him away or ignore him. There is a civilised stand-off which is perfect. He has gone pretty quiet since we all got here which is perfect too, much better than him being all fake and sucking up to adults. My guess is that he doesn't have any friends who are girls, because the boarding school abroad that he and Alex go to is for boys only. Gussy couldn't believe that when he heard it and thought it was in a country where 'girls are illegal' – he *actually* said that. The idea that people might choose to be educated with only their own gender was beyond him. Now every time he asks for something, like a phone or a glass of orange juice we tell him it's illegal. Gussy is good value, but I still wish Nick were staying here instead.

Ro got all sensible with us about an hour ago and said we had to start to get used to getting up early as we'll have six am starts in a day or so. Gussy thinks she is joking so we played along and told him that he'd be allowed sleep in until eleven, that the early starts were for the less important people, not for stars like him.

DAY
FOURTEEN

I almost wish the film crew wasn't coming tomorrow,
I'm loving being here without them. It's now early
afternoon and we are all (except Ro) sprawled around
the huge sitting room, which is like three sitting
rooms all under one very moulded ceiling, hiding out
from a rain shower. Stephen and Paul are playing
chess in one section, the girls and their magazines
are with me here on the other side of the room, Alex
is lying on the middle sofa telling some hellishly long
story to Gussy about a commercial he once appeared
in, and Gussy is pretending to follow.

Even in such a short time we have become a little family with Ro like the efficient working mother, Paul like the fun dad always having ideas for games and parties, Stephen like the gangly, distant old uncle, Lorna like the stroppy older daughter, Alice the sweet little girl, Gussy and Alex like the troublesome little boys. I don't know what that makes *me* though.

I just ran this notion past Lorna and Alice who both said, 'The Governess', at the exact same time. Scary!

It's been pretty interesting so far today. This morning Ro and I were up first and she raced off on her bike to the current location to help Bob organise the move to this one, which left me wandering the grounds alone again.

Determined not to turn into The Bird Lady Of The Grange, I went exploring. There's a tiny one-room cottage with two cobwebbed windows sitting behind the rose bushes, which you can't see from the main house thanks to the tall hedge. An idea came to me that maybe it would be a good place to go and write my journal once the hordes arrive tomorrow. Just as I was tugging away at the latch, a hand appeared from out of nowhere and landed on mine. I nearly jumped out of my body with fright as I'd been so lost in thought that I hadn't heard a soul. It was Stephen, looking extra geeky as he had bed-head to beat the band and glasses on that are even worse than mine, (*his* Dad probably didn't see reports about possible blindness through contact lens abuse the way mine did).

At first I was furious, assuming he was trying to stop me looking inside the cottage, but then I realised he wanted to help. The door was wedged closed by a bent-over nail, which puzzled Stephen as he insisted that he'd stored a broken chair inside the cottage only last week. I suggested that maybe Bob had asked Ro to do it for safety. After five minutes of trying to wrench it free using stones, bits of wood, and even the arm of his glasses and my fountain pen, we gave up and headed away from the cottage.

Stephen didn't say anything at all as we walked back towards the hedge. The silence thing is getting a bit creepy. I suppose he doesn't think I'm worth talking to, which is nuts because he talks to Paul and my brother is certainly no conversational prize. And it can't be that he's nervous of me because he's known me for years, since I ran around dressed head-to-toe in yellow and purple. I even used to have a pencil-sharpener collection that he knows about.

That could account for it, actually.

Not that I mind, it's just annoying when someone who isn't as cool as you are doesn't like you. And there are precious few people less cool than me so it feels like a bit of a waste.

As we walked closer to the main house we started to hear loud noises like a clunking of metal. We stopped a moment to listen and then we heard people screaming and both started running back there as fast as we could. Luckily it wasn't a case of 'murder by metal things', they were shrieks of excitement from Lorna and Alice (and I suspect Alex) when several large rails of costumes arrived with one of the wardrobe attendants and some lifting-guys.

Until that moment I hadn't wondered or worried about the costumes, but now I realized that this was what people would see me in, what NICK would see me in, for days on end.

OK, Alice has just fled from the sitting room with Lorna right after her. My guess is she saw people arrive.

LATER

I was right. Amber, Bonnie, Hanna and my cousin Sophie all landed here together for the fitting and all of us girls ran upstairs to the new female extras' wardrobe room (one of the first-floor bedrooms) where the wardrobe girl was still working away arranging things. There are so many rails of costumes, all labelled and being ironed with some kind of high-pressure steam-jet thingy, which I'm sure has a proper name.

The dresses looked stunning, all silk and chiffon, empire-line and floor-length. We hoped we could try on everything in sight, but Lizzy had given them our photos, heights and shoe sizes from the other day so a costume had already chosen for each of us.

I was resigned to looking the worst, as usual, but because of my height I was wearing a dress from the women's section of the wardrobe department and not the girl's section and it looked way better than any of the others. It fitted perfectly. I was told by Wendy (the wardrobe girl who is only about twenty), that it was originally made for a lead actress in a TV movie a couple of years ago and they just spruced it up a bit with an underskirt and dyed it lilac. Apparently they always recycle costumes from movie to movie, altering pieces as they go.

Lorna looks really odd in a dress, as if it's one big itch for her, but Hanna looked amazing – very different, but very lovely, and I think she knew it as she was grinning even as the heavy make-up came off and the newly dark-brown hair was uncovered from under her beanie. Sophie, Alice, Amber and Bonnie all look good, but their costumes are a bit ordinary compared to the others so Wendy says she'll fix that by tomorrow.

The shoes were another matter. They hurt. No wonder people died sooner in those days, they wanted to leave the planet to get away from the constant foot pain they were in. Wendy says that the trick is to bring sneakers onto the set, have your shoes in a draw-string bag and then change into them at the last minute, and that I could put my glasses in there at the last minute too. She wanted to have me wear this hat thing, but I begged her with just my eyes and she put it away with a smile, and replaced it with this large hair-ornament that she came across in some box. It looked like a plain, silver, spidery shape with lots of glass blobs, but she bent it so two of the prongs could fasten in my hair and spruced it up with a ribbon covering the glass bits so it's not so shiny, and added two feathers and now it looks amazing. She then tied a similar piece of ribbon around my wrist and it really works. Wendy in wardrobe is going to be a very cool person to have around.

Once we were sorted Wendy disappeared next door to fit out the guys.

As we reluctantly, and not so reluctantly (Lorna), got changed back into our usual clothes everyone was telling me that mine was the best and I was trying to tell them great things about theirs, but I couldn't help smiling all the same.

Pretty soon we could hear Gussy at the top of his voice going, 'You have GOT to be joking! I play football you know, give that to Alex!' and Paul who was obviously dancing about the room la-la-ing the tune to an old-fashioned waltz.

Lorna and Hanna suggested we peep in at the keyhole, but the rest of us didn't think we could ever recover from such a thing in our own lifetimes. Good thing we nixed that plan as we met Nick and the other three guys coming up the stairs, but they didn't have time to talk as they were late for the fitting. I think the others are called Owen and Pete and Fraser, but I might have that wrong because they are from Paul's class in school and don't come round to the house much. Nick avoided eye-contact with me completely when he said 'Hi'.

Stephen invited the others to hang out here after the fittings and they're around until tonight so the place has that summer camp feel. I am now hiding out in my window-sill nook in the library and can hear the guys and Lorna, Hanna and Alice next door in the billiards room. I am determined not to go and find Nick, he can come and find me. I think he still owes me an apology for the dance thing. And a social life. And a year or two.

LATER STILL

It's about eleven at night and I know this means I'm going to be exhausted in the morning, but I don't think I'll sleep until I get it all out.

I thought this was going to be one of the best days ever and it turned out to be awful. It was *exactly* like that Christmas when I wanted a puppy and got pyjamas and a lamp. Of course I waited *endlessly* for Nick, or anyone, to come looking for me, and they all just left me alone reading in the library. Soon my leg fell asleep from sitting in an appealing-looking position. Honestly! I could have slipped down a well or been knocked unconscious by a falling jar of goose grease in one of the pantries, but they wouldn't have found me until I was inches from death and then they'd have had to sit quietly around the billiards room with Alice crying and all of them saying lovely things about me. OK Lemony, reel it in! Point being, they *totally* didn't miss me or want me around.

I was pretty miserable by the time the gong sounded in the hallway for dinner. Because there were so many of us Miss Higgins had pizzas delivered. I tried to get in a good mood again, but you know what it's like when you've been sulking for ages, it's hard to just snap out of it because it feels like someone owes you something first.

Before long the sixteen of us were in the large basement kitchen with veggie pizzas, a sound system and a real party going. Professor Brown looked in and seemed surprised to find anyone in his house, but soon remembered and, nodding and smiling, went back upstairs to his more civilised existence. My dark mood lifted slightly, but not enough that I was talking or dancing much. Ro and Alice both came over and gave me a hug, I know they think it's because of Nick and Donna, but really it's just that I feel like I never really fit in. It's fine when it's just a handful of people, but as soon as there are loads I feel as if I am all wrong somehow, a lemon hanging from an apple tree.

The eight who aren't sleeping here left a couple of hours ago and we 'Grangers' as Ro says the rest of the film crew has started calling us, went up to bed. Before undressing I suddenly remembered that I'd left this in the window nook in the library and considering how I'd go into a spontaneous coma if anyone found and read the terrible truth that is my life right now, it needed rescuing.

My plan was to fetch it and get straight back to bed, but while I was there in the library I heard a noise in the courtyard outside. The lights were off so I could pull back the velvet curtain and see a woman with blonde hair and a man's coat wrapped almost double around her as she ran across the courtyard to where a small, thin man (much smaller than the Professor) was standing with a flashlight in his hand. They crept off together towards the grounds and for some reason I ran downstairs, out the ballroom door at the side and followed them into the night. I could see the light from the torch, but lost my nerve when I saw them disappear around the side of the large hedge. Going back inside and telling myself it was probably Bob and a member of the crew checking things out for tomorrow, I ran as quietly as I could back upstairs and am now in the girls' bathroom writing this and getting a grip. That's the problem with an over-active imagination, you turn a bog-standard person with a flashlight into a murderous fiend with fiendishly murderous plans. Drama is *so* my thing. Say, goodnight, Lemony.

DAY FIFTEEN

But then why were they running? And why so quiet and nervous looking? Ro was up and out before all of us, so I didn't get to ask her opinion.

The big news of the day so far: first thing this morning I got showered and dressed and bumped into NICK!!! on my way back to the bedroom. He was on his way to wake up the rest of the boys and explained that his dad had dropped him off early. Having flashed my best smile I was so cool with him, said I'd see him later and breezed back into the bedroom only to catch sight of the mirror and the reflection of my smug little head complete with *shower cap still on it*. Only *I* could manage to make such a complete fool of myself with the guy I have been in love with for two years even before most people in the land are awake. I am *such* an over-achiever!

I am hoping against hope that he found it adorable. No, I am hoping against *all reason* that he found it adorable.

Our cosy 'family' breakfasts are a thing of the past. The place was already milling with dozens of people. I felt as if they'd all invaded my house and it isn't even my house. By the time I wandered outside I realised there were at least a hundred bodies running around looking either busy or lost. I hadn't expected so many. The courtyard, driveway and one of the lawns were packed tightly with vans, trucks, cars and caravans. Ro says not to call them caravans, to call them trailers or Winnebagoes. There wasn't much time to talk to her as she was running around and adults were coming up to her to ask her questions about where to put things. But she did tell me that Bob wasn't there last night.

Because all of us girls and some of the guys are under sixteen, we need a chaperone for legal reasons, someone to keep watch over us on set. I was worried that it would be a school teacher kind of person determined not to let us have any fun. The best news is that Miss Higgins has been given the job of chaperone! She told us last night and said that we could look after ourselves and she'd be there if we needed her. We were also warned that if we caused any trouble then she'd have to start to supervise us more closely. Lizzie is doubling as the assistant chaperone and warned us that if we upset her she'll get Wendy from wardrobe to put us into hideous outfits and make sure we were at the front of each shot.

I went to report to Lizzie as Miss Higgins had told us to, and she pointed out this sort of catering van where people were lining up to get served breakfast. I wasn't ready to eat, but felt I should. Then another person (I had no idea who anyone was) showed me a parked double-decker bus and said to eat in there. It had little rectangular café-tables inside and bus-type seats and to my relief Paul bounded on and sat beside me to eat.

I wanted to tell him about the two people acting strangely in the courtyard last night, and maybe chat about how different it was with all these people, but he just sat down with his breakfast and opened with, 'I'm in love with Ro.'

He just out and said it, no lead up, no hints-and-maybes for a couple of weeks, not even, 'You know your best friend Ro, yeah?' or anything like that, just 'I'm in love with Ro.' I didn't know how to take it, it was like my brain melted slowly. My brother feeling that way about my best friend!

So I snapped, 'Well, she's too busy today to be in love back, so finish your eggs.'

'Fair enough,' he shrugged and kept smiling.

I couldn't believe it, I was so angry. I know she has no clue about all this as she would have told me. If Paul and Ro end up going out with each other then I will be *completely* the outsider, I won't belong anywhere! I wolfed down the rest of my food, stormed off the dining bus and ran straight into Stephen who was wearing a regency soldier's uniform. We collided so hard that my glasses bumped against his chin and it looked really sore. I just kept saying 'sorry' over and over as I walked away.

Then Gussy and Nick were standing right behind him, also wearing infantry uniforms and Nick laughed and said, 'Oh look, is that your costume, Lemony? I didn't know there were geeks in those days.'

By then I was wearing just my usual jeans and

what I thought was a really nice top. The ridiculous thing is that part of me was thrilled that he used my name even though he was insulting me! Everything in my life had unravelled within five minutes. I felt like I'd lost my brother, my best friend and all hope of Nick, all without even trying.

The one time I really needed to be on my own and there were swarms of people everywhere I looked. I tried to escape into the library, but the door to that and the billiards room have been locked and every other room is full of equipment and people.

Eventually Hanna and Sophie (who is thrilled that Hanna is hanging out with her even though Sophie is three years younger) dragged me off to get changed into our dresses and since then we've had five hours of doing nothing, waiting to be called on set. Right now I am back in the bedroom where Lorna and Alice are in their costumes and fast asleep, relying on me to wake them whenever we're needed.

From up here I can see most of the other teenagers rushing around outside. They all seem so happy hanging out and getting to know new people and I just feel so closed down. I felt really beautiful in this lilac dress yesterday and today it just makes me feel like a fraud, an ugly duckling who everyone will laugh at in her swan's clothes. I know I'll look all wrong on set and the director will put me sitting behind a tree or something.

I have to go now as Miss Higgins has just called us to go into hair and make-up.

I'm in a movie and I'm miserable. Life is weird.

LATER

It's now late at night and I'm on the large staircase writing this so I don't wake anyone up. The day got much better and I stopped being such a misery to be around. I usually don't wear make-up and it was incredible how they managed to make me look like a real person. The hairdresser and make-up artist, Dipti, made a huge fuss of my hair and spent ages doing a great 'up' hairstyle, set off with the hair-ornament, which she says she'll teach me so I can start doing it myself. My glasses and huge anorak and oldest sneakers kind of ruined the whole effect, but once on set with no glasses and the right shoes I fancied myself as quite presentable. Alice told me that she caught Nick staring at me, and Amber said that the older extras in her 'clump' on set were commenting on me and thought I was one of the real actors!

The afternoon was pretty tiring, walking around as if we were in a park on a Sunday afternoon. When they yelled 'Cut!' we could stop walking and when they yelled, 'Places please!' we had to go back to the beginning to get ready to do it all again. My feet have huge blisters, which the set-nurse has put plasters and ointment on. Wendy was horrified and is finding me new shoes for tomorrow.

Gussy was hugely disappointed that they don't actually say, 'Lights, camera, action!' on a film set after all, but 'Rolling, speed and action', instead. He feels a little short-changed by the whole experience especially as they wouldn't let him 'have a go of the camera'.

At lunchtime everyone stops and all the extras and crew eat on the two dining buses while the actors eat in their trailers. Alex warned us not to go up to the lead actors or ask for photos or autographs, although he's having fun hanging out with them himself. I bet he introduces Lorna to them as a way of making her like him. Miss Higgins says, 'People are people', which I think means that the people you are with are just as important as film stars.

I saw Ro and Paul talking and it all seems like normal so I'm hoping that his love thing is a temporary insanity brought about by the wearing of romantic soldier garb.

DAY SIXTEEN

Today was pretty much identical to yesterday except my feet no longer hurt. Nick looked at me seven-and-a-half times. Paul and Ro are being the same as usual so I'm starting to think that Paul just meant that Ro had done something cool when he said he was in love with her. I mean, anyway, you don't skip straight to love, there are stages: you have to get the hots for someone, then fancy them, then yearn for them, then realise who they are at a soul level, then and only *then* can you think about calling it love. You have to put some money into it too, buy things to impress them before calling it love. I'm not even sure if I'm joking here.

The extras were 'wrapped' (aka finished and sent home) early at around five today, which meant Nick was gone for the evening, and Ro got the night off so she was with the rest of us. Miss Higgins asked us to keep out of the way in the house as the director needed absolute quiet for a scene with two of the leads in the rose garden.

That's how the eight Grangers ended up in the large sitting room again this evening, which was no longer sheltering adult extras, but still had the big signs that Ro had put on the doors about no tea and coffee and taking off your shoes before entering. Miss Higgins had set up a buffet for us at the far end of the room, and when Stephen locked the door we all felt ourselves heave a huge sigh of relief.

Paul had this idea about turning out the lights and telling ghost stories. The room had a magical feel to it, especially after Stephen found these old silver candlesticks, placed them around the room and lit the candles. Paul told 'his' ghost story, which Ro and I have heard a thousand times. Then Alex told a story that he swears is true about a car running on empty because a child needed rescuing from an earthquake in the middle of the night. Lorna and Alice almost told a story between them, but neither could remember the ending. Gussy told a story about a guy he worked with last summer and it was slightly interesting, but not scary as he forgot it was ghost stories we were telling.

Much to everyone's surprise Stephen volunteered to go next. He explained that his was a true story and (probably unlike Alex's one) we could check it out in a book in the library.

'When The Grange was built three hundred years ago, a young woman came to stay here,' he began, and it became obvious that he could tell a good story so we settled down to listen. 'She would spend most of her days reading in the library,' he continued, 'and no one paid much attention to her until one day she began to speak in this weird language no one could understand. She acted perfectly normally apart from these strange words, which she didn't seem to realise she was saying. Her sister came to visit and see if she could help, and she noticed that the young woman was wearing an unusual necklace with a huge diamond and ten smaller diamonds in a circle around it, a necklace that the sister had never seen before. When they tried to take the necklace from the young woman's throat she went into a frenzy of spitting and cursing and scratching at them. They called in the local holy-man who did everything in his power, but all that happened was that the clear diamond in the centre of the necklace started to shudder and turn cloudy and dark.'

At this point it was too scary for Alice who said she needed to use the bathroom anyway and got the key from Stephen to leave the room, locking it behind her as she went.

'Er, we're locked in now,' said Ro, and the guys started making horror sounds.

I was desperate to hear the rest of the story and urged Stephen to go on.

'For ninety days and nights it continued until the young woman suddenly returned to normal, with no recollection of the previous three months, and the diamond turned clear once more. The only thing that she would acknowledge was that she had hidden the diamond necklace for safe keeping, and she said nothing about why the shape of the pendant part of the necklace with the large stone surrounded by ten smaller ones was burned into the palm of her hand. The woman went on marry the heir to the estate and lived to be a hundred years old. During that time people began to believe her claim that if the necklace was ever taken from The Grange then the building would fall to the ground, like with the ravens in the Tower Of London. On her deathbed she confessed that she herself had buried the diamond necklace somewhere in The Grange to be sure the house would always be safe. Her grand-daughter went to fetch pen and paper so she could draw a map, but when she returned the frail old woman was speaking in the same strange language as years before, talking faster and faster until she could no longer breathe, and she died right there on the spot, and the secret of the cursed necklace was buried with her on the grounds of the estate.'

'Where on the grounds?' asked Paul excitedly.

'I bet she's buried in the utility room,' Lorna piped up. 'There's a funny smell from there.'

I was too involved in the story to notice until then that Ro was gripping on to Paul's sleeve really tightly from fear, or from something anyway.

Then Alice returned and insisted we turn the lights back on, closely followed by Ro reminding us we need to get some sleep.

I guess that means me too.

DAY SEVENTEEN

I was so tired today from staying awake to write, and my hoped-for morning nap didn't happen as they were ready to shoot almost immediately after breakfast. The monotony of doing the same thing over and over was relieved to some extent by chatting with some of the adult extras and Sophie who was also in my group of 'walkers' today. Sophie was a bit annoyed that none of the other teens were in our group and also that she has to wear this white sort of cap that children wore in those days while we all get to look more like young adults.

We were all talking about the fact that someone broke into the trailer of one of the lead actors, we think it was Antonia's, but no one is saying for sure. Apparently nothing was taken, but the police came around to check it out anyway. Gussy thought the police were extras dressed up, not thinking that perhaps their 'costumes' might be from the wrong century.

At lunch, Nick was visible from my viewpoint beside Wendy, Lizzie, and Sophie. No one was fooled by my pretending to listen as my focus was on the blonde lady talking to Nick who I suddenly realised was the woman I'd seen in the courtyard that night. When I went to fetch dessert for me and Sophie, Nick was there too and I asked, 'You know that blonde lady you were talking to, what does she do here?'

And instead of the answer I expect like, 'Oh, she's one of the lighting crew,' or whatever, he started saying, 'Oh, *jealous* are we?' and really making fun of me.

For the first time ever I was glad to see Stephen who came over and told Nick he was needed by Lizzy.

LATER

I can hear the click of billiard balls, but the door is

locked so I'm guessing he's hiding out there. I didn't mean to insult him, I just wanted him to swap partners.

Earlier, just after we wrapped, Lizzy told us that for the next few days of ballroom scenes she was pairing us up with each other. She automatically put Lorna with Alex, much to his delight, Alice and Paul were cool with being put together, and then she told me that Stephen would be my partner, which makes sense because of the height thing. Sophie almost cried because she isn't considered old enough to dance in the scenes and has to sit with two old lady extras. When Bonnie found out she'd be paired with Nick she came rushing over to me saying she'd be happy to switch. Nick doesn't know yet as he'd gone home by the time Lizzy made the announcement. Lizzy said the switch was fine as long as Nick was the same height as me or taller and if Stephen didn't mind, but he'd wandered off by then so I had to go find him.

I figured Stephen couldn't possibly have a problem with it as Bonnie is way more fabulous than me, and her peach dress looks like a red-carpet thumbs-up after what Wendy did with it. With this all making perfect sense to me I took myself off to ask Stephen to be Bonnie's partner for the next few days instead of mine.

I thought maybe I hadn't made myself clear as he just stared at me, so I began to talk through it again when he stopped me and said, 'I got it the first time,' and stalked off, no doubt to ask his dad for the keys to the billiards room. I'll just hang out here and explain the background history (or lack of) between me and Nick, although he must be the only person on set, or in this town even, who is not yet aware of the fact.

STILL LATER

I was sitting on the stairs writing when Stephen stormed out of the billiards room, and as soon as he saw me he marched into his dad's office and came out with two sheets of paper. He sat down on the step above mine and handed me the paper.

'I'd like you to do something for me, Lemony,' he said. His voice was steady, but kind of strained. 'I know you like writing. I'd like you to write down everything I've ever done wrong to make you hate me so much. I've been trying to work it out, but as far as I can tell I've only ever been nice to you and helpful, so I need you to put it on paper for me. I may not be able to joke about and dance around the way your brother and the other guys can, but I don't think that's reason enough to get all snappy with me and pull away every time I walk into a room. I don't understand and I like to understand things so please do me this one favour and I promise I will stay far away from you for the rest of the summer.'

I felt completely stunned so I just took the paper from him and as he walked off, I blurted, 'It's just that you speak Chinese and picked the onion bits out of the quiche.'

He looked really angry with me although his voice was still calm as he said, 'I can't help speaking Chinese and I get severely embarrassed when my dad shows it off like I'm some prize pig, sometimes to the point of merely being able to sit there and grin like an idiot. And I'm *so* allergic to eating onions that my face and hands turn red and blow up like a puffer-fish, so I was either in a position of offending your mum's cooking or ending up in a hospital or a freak show. Lemony, I know I don't exactly fit in sometimes, it's just that I don't have any brothers or sisters, and at school I'm working so hard to keep my scholarship that I don't have time to hang out and party like Alex. I really hope that Chinese and onions aren't my only crimes.'

I might have seen the beginnings of smile but I couldn't be sure.

And he was gone.

I know he's been really annoying me, but I didn't think it showed. If I'm honest it's that he reminds me of myself so much and I don't really like being me. I sat there for about five minutes feeling sort of sick and hating myself, especially since his chin had been all bruised from where my glasses hit against him yesterday. When other people are mean to someone I'm always the first to stick up for them and now I realise that *I've* been the horrible one.

I went back upstairs to the attic and Lorna was still awake. She's not a girl to pull her punches so I asked, 'What do you think of Stephen?'

'Stephen? Why? He's cool.' Lorna is not as fluent in girl-talk as the rest of us.

I was hoping she'd say he was really annoying or geeky or something so I'd feel better, but instead she said, 'He's much more mature than the rest of them, and more intelligent.' By then she was on a roll. 'He always notices other people and how they're feeling, like yesterday he went and gave your cousin Sophie a hug because he could tell she was hating having to do the scene over and over and feeling left out when we were laughing about that time with Dairne at the café.'

'Who are we talking about?' Alice was now awake.

'Stephen,' Lorna said, 'Lemony wants to know what I think of him.'

'Just because I don't really know him as much as I know everyone else,' I said way too quickly.

'Stephen?' Ro now joined in.

'Lemony wants to know him better,' Alice explained.

'Is that so?'

'Forget it!' I said, 'Goodnight.'

Now they all think I have gone off Nick and am into Stephen, which is not true, but is a lot less embarrassing than the truth.

DAY EIGHTEEN

I skipped the dining bus at breakfast this morning and instead brought Wendy a cup of tea and a bourbon cream up to the wardrobe room. She could tell this was code for needing to chat.

'I've been horrible to someone,' I explained.

'On purpose?' she asked, losing half her biscuit in the first dunk.

'No. But that doesn't make it any easier for the other person,' I sighed.

'True. You're a smart girl, what are you going to do about it?

'No idea. I guess I'm not smart when it comes to the stuff that counts.'

'Well, Lemony, the tea and biscuit thing is making *me* feel great.'

'Give him a cup of tea and a biscuit? Like a symbolic peace offering? I have always said that there's not much in this world that can't be healed with a jammy dodger.'

'That's my girl!'

Problem was that by the time I got back outside Stephen was standing beside Nick, but I was determined to be a better person and marched over with the tea and three of the more interesting biscuits from the kraft-table selection and handed them to a rather surprised Stephen. They both looked puzzled for a moment, but then Stephen nodded and smiled. Then Nick took the biscuits from him, which wasn't supposed to happen, but Stephen kept smiling so I felt better. I also handed him the two pieces of paper which were folded small against prying eyes. The word 'sorry' is written on one, and the word 'very' on the other.

The scene we were shooting today involved us all sitting on garden chairs as if watching an outdoor concert and I was in a position where I could stare at

Nick between takes. I am actually getting paid for gawking at Nick Collins all day, but also getting a bit bored with him. I've never been in his company for long enough to realise that he has so very little to say. Today he talked about sports results and made fun of other people and that was it. Still, maybe I can be the interesting one in the relationship and he can be the fun one. And Donna can do what? Fetch us snacks? Keep forgetting about her.

We wrapped at a sensible time and I'm in bed early, and vowing to be less of a reason for people to want to shut themselves away with billiards. What is a billiard anyway, I mean when it's not doing the plural thing?

DAY NINETEEN

Nick is no longer on the film! He was warned by Lizzy more than once about twitching around and drawing attention to himself when the cameras were rolling, and apparently last night Julian, the director, decided he'd had enough. Major! Even all the adults are talking about it. In fact Wendy told me first, but not until I was in my new white ball gown for the dancing scenes, which showed that she knows what I'm like.

Alex asked his dad if Nick could have some other off-camera job, but his Dad said that if Nick didn't have the self-discipline to be an extra then he wouldn't be considered for any other job either. Paul, Ro, Miss Higgins and pretty much everyone including Lizzy and Bob (who Ro must have told) came over to make sure I was going to stay on the film.

I am going to stick with it because I said I'd do the job, and because I really want to be here. The thought of Nick hanging out with Donna every day isn't bugging me as much as I thought it would. I'm a bit ashamed of him really, and that's saying something if you consider I didn't even feel shame that time he ate tar for a dare.

All that banishment and drama-drama, and the fact that Fraser left when Nick did, meant that the dancing partners all had to be swapped around anyway. Lizzie was having a stressy day and just looked at the clump of us teenagers as if we were a pile of unscaled fish, and said, 'Oh sort yourselves out.'

So in an act of fine diplomacy I stood beside Stephen who actually had the nerve to laugh at me, but then asked, 'Would you care to dance Miss Smith?'

I replied, 'That's remarkably forward of you, Mr

Brown. However, I would love to dance on the understanding that you shall keep your hands where a gentleman ought.'

'I shall struggle to comply,' he smiled.

He was an OK dancer (compared to Gussy and Paul at least) and my feet and my dignity survived, so all good there then.

The guys all looked amazing in their dress uniforms and I asked Stephen if he thought my ivory ballgown suited me.

'Em, yes ... yes, very much,' he said, sounding surprised.

I have a theory than you can tell what kind of person a guy is by the length of pause he takes before lying to you about how you look. Too short a pause and he's a habitual liar, too long a pause and he doesn't care enough about you to make up something good quickly. Stephen's pause was just the right length. I told him my theory and thanked him for his gentlemanly dishonesty, and then the first AD yelled 'Places!' so we had to concentrate.

This afternoon one of the older extras was given a line to say, and he was ridiculously excited about it because he is usually a plumber with dreams of escaping to Hollywood or the RSC. Hanna and I helped him learn his one short line for four hours, which probably means that he will remain a plumber and not be in the Shakespeare festival any year soon. Sophie is now cool about not dancing because she was heavily featured in a shot where she had to act with the lead character, helping her to re-tie a ribbon at the back of her dress. I just contacted Mum to make sure they all make a fuss and phone her.

It's starting to feel like home around here. A circus style of living, but a good one once you know what's what. I have worked out that biscuits are the currency on set. This is because they both feed your stomach and your need for something new to do. There are two classes of biscuits, good biscuits and boring ones, and if you have a stash of the good stuff then people need you. You have the power to withhold or bestow, to please or disappoint, to feed or to starve, and that is the kind of power that kings themselves would envy. The stocks are replenished at the tea and coffee table twice a day, but I've become friends with John and Caro on the catering crew and they let me pillage in advance. I would have been *so* good in the Second World War, I would have controlled all lines of supplies and communication, I would have outwitted *everyone* and kept Europe for myself. Proof? I have five custard creams and two chocolate chips right now hidden in my woolly hat. Which I am not right now wearing. Naturally.

Shouldn't have written about biscuits, now I'm hungry.

script

DAY TWENTY

Today was a day off for everyone except the security guards, which gave the place an abandoned look after the hordes of the last few days. I was determined to get up and out to the little cottage for a snoop around, but was prevented by three things.

One: Exhaustion, I didn't wake until nine.

Two: Pancakes, blueberry, too delicious to rush especially as it was only me, Ro and Paul in the dining room staring quietly and comfortably into nothing but maple syrup and recovering from the madness of recent days.

Three: My own mother, who showed up to take me into town, thus reminding me about the whole morning at the wall, which now makes me laugh when I think of it.

It's fantastic news, she has decided that I am allowed to join the twenty-first century after all and have a shot at an actual normal life. While writing this I have been blinking four times more than usual thanks to the brand new contact lenses in my eyes. Luckily mine is a straightforward prescription. I think Miss Higgins had a word with her when she phoned to make sure myself and Paul hadn't become complete delinquents yet.

The lenses are great, but *this* was so mortifying – as soon as we got back to The Grange Mum got talking to Professor Brown and they both had this great idea of having Stephen show me how to look after my lenses. I explained that the woman in the opticians had already taken me through it, but they insisted, and a rather confused-looking Stephen ended up going up the attic stairs with me towards the bathrooms.

He suddenly turned around and said, 'Lemony, this is just our parents being weird, right? You don't need me to show you this, do you?'

'No, I know what to do, it's not exactly rocket science.'

'Good', he said, 'I want to show you something.'

And with that he started bounding down the stairs to the library.

Over the fireplace hangs a large, old family portrait, which I'd seen a dozen times, but hadn't wondered about.

'That's her, the woman who wore the diamond necklace and spoke in tongues,' Stephen said, pointing to the woman in the red dress in the centre. 'She isn't wearing the necklace, of course, she sat for the painting later in her life.'

Around her were gathered other men and women each holding something like a fan, a book, a hunting rifle, as Stephen explained, an object of value or significance to them. Only that lady sat with her arms empty. It was strange because although her hands were folded in her lap, they seemed to be pointing towards something, as if her index finger was made of wood or she wanted the painter to notice someone who'd walked into the room.

'The other night I mentioned to my father that I'd told you all the story of the lady of the necklace,' Stephen continued, 'And he asked me if I knew that this was her. It's funny how I've known the story and the painting since I was small and never put the two together. And I now I desperately want to know ...'

'... what is she pointing to and where is the necklace?' I finished for him.

'Exactly,' he grinned, 'I knew you'd understand.'

What I do *not* understand is how a sixteen-year-old guy can refer to his dad as his 'father', but hey.

Just then Ro bounced into the room, which was weird as she hasn't spent any time in the library as far as I know, closely followed by Paul, which wasn't so weird giving his current affliction. Instead of being pleased to see me Ro headed straight for Stephen and demanded to be told what was going on.

'He was just showing me the painting of the lady with the necklace,' I blurted.

But she didn't mean what was going on with me and Stephen being there, she was talking about what the security guards had told her.

'I just spoke with Security, and they say they're not allowed to tell, but that you might know something. Stephen! You know I'll find out so you might as well tell me now,' Ro used her dog-training tone which made Stephen stare at her with a mixture of amusement and concern, as if she was some chainsaw-wielding child.

Stephen motioned for us to sit on the large leather

chairs as he stood at the fireplace to surrender his story.

'There have been several break-ins during the past few days, not just the one in the actor's trailer. This library, the utility room and my father's office have been searched. Nothing was taken, but the locks were tampered with and a window in one of the kitchens was broken.'

'I knew it!' said Ro.

He then looked at us for an age on the edge of his next sentence, finally deciding to let it out.

'I think they're looking for the diamond necklace, whoever "they" might be.'

'How can they be looking for the necklace if we're the only ones who know about it?' Ro asked, and it seemed a sensible question.

Twice in my life my brother has surprised me, once when he confessed his love for Ro and again when he said, 'The script for the film is partly based on the story, so the rumour has been about for weeks.'

We never even saw a script, in fact I totally forgot that there might be one.

'And it wouldn't be difficult to research it,' Stephen added, 'In fact many people in the film industry realise that the story of the necklace is why Alex's dad was interested in filming at The Grange in the first place.'

It seemed like a good time to share my middle-of-the-night adventure with the blonde woman and the man the night before the crew arrived with them, and we began to discuss it from all possible angles. It must have been hours, but it seemed like only minutes before Miss Higgins came to call us to join the others for dinner in the kitchen. They were all talking about Nick and Fraser, and laughing about their own attempts at dancing in the ballroom scenes, while the four of us stayed lost in our hopes of finding a clue that might shed some light on things. Ro hardly ate a thing and stared out into the middle distance. Yeah. It's all gone a bit Sherlock Holmes around here, but that's not a bad thing I suppose.

Mental as it may be, I do believe that if the necklace is taken off the grounds this place won't survive.

whatever

DAY TWENTY-ONE

News of the day – the lead actress is sick with the flu (or maybe she has her own Nick and Donna thing that needs to be avoided!) so they are filming in another location with a reduced crew and hope to start back here again in a couple of days.

Lorna, Alice, and Gussy have gone home until then, and Alex has a room in the hotel suite with his dad. So that leaves only me and Ro in one room and Stephen and Paul in the other. Which suits me perfectly as I have a lot of catching up to do with Ro, and the only guy who is not my brother is completely harmless so I won't have to watch what I look like. In fact today I'm wearing jeans, one of Lorna's sweaters which looks as odd on me as it would on her if she ever wore it, and my glasses again as I'm not supposed to wear my lenses for long until my eyes get used to them. In short, I look as scruffy today as I've been looking elegant on set. I am definitely having a 'before picture' day.

Paul and Ro had a competition at breakfast to see who could eat kippers in the most creative way. Paul won, but I won't write how he did it in case someone finds this and tries to copy him and dies.

The rest of breakfast was quite civilised if you don't count the number of waffles I put away. Nothing could be said with Miss Higgins around, not that she'd be one to climb in a smashed kitchen window at three in the morning, but you just never can tell.

The library seemed to be the obvious place to start, and the back of the painting the most obvious place to look. While we were busy being obvious Paul actually said, 'I wonder if we'll solve the mystery and save the day.'

He sang the Scooby Doo music until Ro asked him to stop. Now that *really* worried me, the fact that she *asked* him, I mean when did she stop thumping him over things?

The picture wouldn't budge, in fact we discovered it was nailed tight to the wall. On examining the edges it became clear that it must have been that way for years, the layers of paint coming just up to the frame.

Stephen was the only one of us not to be disappointed.

'Don't you see? This means that it was fixed there centuries ago and must be pointing to something in this room.'

Right at that moment Ro was standing in the path of the pointing finger and laughed, 'Don't stitch *me* up, pointy lady!

But when she moved it was clear that portrait was indicating towards a waist-high, bronze statue of a young man wearing a short tunic.

Stephen stepped forward and checked around it.

'I know for a fact that this statue doesn't move from its base, so it must have been fixed in that position. It's the reason we have rugs in here instead of carpets.'

There didn't seem to be anything remarkable about the statue.

'Who is it supposed to be anyway?' asked Paul,

disappointed. 'He looks a little under-dressed to be a Brown.'

'Theseus,' said Stephen staring hard, as if the statue would start to whisper its secrets if we wanted it enough.

'Who's Theseus?' asked Ro.

'A Greek hero who proved himself by lifting a huge, enormous boulder when he was sixteen.' I explained.

'God, that is *such* a guy move,' she grinned.

'Lifted a boulder ... maybe ... Got any large rocks lying about the place, Stephen?' For the first time since discovering the painting was fixed, Paul seemed to wake up and care about more than simply standing a bit too close to Ro.

'Yes,' something was dawning on Stephen, 'Yes, there's a huge boulder near the orchard now that you mention it. I used to sit on it to read *The Iliad* when I was younger.'

'*The Iliad*? Too much information, Stevey Babe,' Paul shook his head in mock angst and led the way out the door.

Unfortunately it had begun to pour with rain, the kind of rain that you couldn't stand up in, the kind that would make you think of donating money to a flood charity, just in case. So we stayed in.

Paul decided to teach Ro to play chess, which is as dangerous as teaching anyone else to drive. I left the sitting room when the second rook went sailing past my head. I came up here to the library to write this and was surprised to find Stephen here as usually the place is all mine. He's had his head buried in several large reference books and doesn't look set to join the real world again any time soon. I think he's forgotten I'm here.

LATER

Or not. That was so weird, as soon as I wrote that last sentence he looked up and said, 'Lemony, I think I've found something. Tell me what you notice about this.'

The book was ancient and the size of a small coffee table, and was an illustrated history of The Grange. It had plans and blueprints and whatever from the first hundred years of the house. I wished I'd put my contacts in (as if they would make me see things that my head was too slow to notice).

'Is the little cottage missing? Or did it used to be round like that?' I guessed.

'I think that round thing is the boulder – look there's no boulder where it is today ... my guess is that the boulder was moved and the cottage built on the exact spot where it used to be. Which means the necklace could be hidden in the cottage.'

That's one cool thing about Stephen, I actually sometimes have to put in a bit of an effort to keep up.

'Stephen, if this is true then someone else is onto it! Remember we couldn't open the cottage door because someone had made a lock with a six-inch nail.'

I stopped just long enough to throw this under a chair as Stephen and I both raced for the door and outside into the rain, which had gone from being outrageous to just unkind. I don't know why we didn't stop for coats or an umbrella, it wasn't as if the cottage was going anywhere, or as if our adventure involved a kidnapped toddler in need of urgent meds.

We were soaked through by the time we rounded the rose garden and reached the cottage door. Stephen was a man on a mission; he grabbed a huge stone and kept bashing at the nail until it gave. Then he pushed and shoved to open the door, as there were planks of wood, a wheelbarrow and a broken chair just inside it. Once we were standing inside the cottage – me upright with my head an inch shy of the ceiling, and Stephen stooping slightly – we laughed at how we were drenched through.

The obvious thing to do was to start searching, hoping there would be something to find.

I'm not sure if it was ten minutes later or a lot longer, and I'm not sure how it happened exactly, but I somehow managed to loosen a high shelf while looking under a tin of paint. In a split second it became a missile, flying sideways off the wall, weighted with half-full tins of paint and carpentry tools, which began falling in all directions. Stephen was lifting something and turned just in time to be hit across the head with the corner of the shelf; as he fell to the floor, several heavy tins and a hammer crashed down onto his chest. I screamed, but he was totally silent. I pushed the debris away from him, tripping over myself with apologies until the sight of the blood dripping from his head made me realise I had to run for help.

As I turned to go he called out. He wouldn't let me leave, and wanted me to stay and help him stand. It took a minute or two, but as soon as he could get up he leaned against me for support and we hobbled back out into the rain. He was swaying and the blood was dripping and dissolving in the puddles as we made our way along the path. I remember saying over and over how sorry I was and he kept wincing and gasping that it would all be all right. Such painfully slow progress. He felt more of the pain and I felt more of the slowness, but eventually we got to the house. By now he was a strange, pale-grey colour and I was so panicked that I'd started to cry. He closed his eyes as he slumped down on the first couch in the smaller sitting room and I ran up to the Professor's office yelling for help all the way.

Soon everyone was around, bending over Stephen, getting me to breathe and calm down, shouting to get a doctor, running for towels and something to stop the bleeding from Stephen's head.

I couldn't even see at that point as my glasses had fallen off at some stage, and I was crying so hard I couldn't explain what had happened. I just remember them saying, 'He's fine' to me over and over, and saying, 'She's fine' to Stephen who obviously never knew me to be capable of having such a complete nervous breakdown and was probably concerned that if I lost any more of the plot I might end up knocking down a chandelier or two and levelling The Grange.

I am writing this from bed since the doctor insisted I rest too, but thought that a cold from the wet clothes was my only danger (I managed to sneak back to the library to fetch this while everyone else was having dinner). Someone went and found my glasses when I was with the doctor, so at least I can see to write.

Stephen had a mild concussion, bruising to his chest, and a head wound that needed four stitches. He is asleep in the room next door and probably won't be waking up until he's twenty and I am long gone from here. Everyone keeps saying it wasn't my fault, but it was, and now he won't be in the film anymore and we'll never find out about the break-ins or the necklace. It feels like the curse of the necklace is coming true piece by piece.

This is *way* beyond the kind of thing that three biscuits and a cup of tea could solve. I usually only ruin dinner, or my chances with Nick, or a joke, or maybe my own reputation as a normal person. This time I have gone and ruined EVERYTHING.

DAY TWENTY-TWO

I woke really late this morning feeling a bit wobbly, and I couldn't face Stephen. I was thinking about moving home, but Professor Brown said that my moving out would make his son feel far worse than a bang on the head would ever do. I told Ro and Paul about what we'd been up to and their take on it was that if Stephen had been there alone the shelf might have fallen anyway, so it was lucky I was there to help. The logic in that is slightly twisted in my favour, but it was lovely of them to want me to feel happier.

Paul said that Stephen slept through the night and Ro visited him after breakfast. Apparently he wants to see me, but I *can't* face him, so I'm going to write him a note and send it in when Miss Higgins brings his lunch.

TWO HOURS LATER

My note to Stephen read:

Dear Mr Brown,

I can only suppose that neither my glasses nor my rude manners were good enough weapons of destruction over the past few days hence my having to resort to the old 'shelf trick'. No doubt I will manage to finish you off completely if I actually ever make you a cup of tea instead of just fetching one. 'Sorry' doesn't cover it. Please let me give you my brother Paul by way of compensation. Really, keep him.

Yours generously,

Miss Lemony Smith.

I also got the reference books from the library, the one with all the plans of The Grange and the others he had piled there, and asked Miss Higgins to deliver those to him.

Miss Higgins came back with a note from him in return that simply said,

I had to assume either the bump on the head had turned him simple or he really wanted to talk to me in a hurry. I knocked nervously on the bedroom door and went in to find him sitting up in bed wearing the kind of traditional blue-striped PJs that I would have expected, a large bandage around his head and his glasses sitting gingerly on his face. He was smiling at me.

'Did you actually make a *plan* to ruin my life or is all this sort of accidental?' he said.

'Half and half,' I shrugged miserably.

He insisted I share his lunch, and because Miss Higgins had provided enough food to explode even a guy's stomach, I thought it would help him if I ate part of the pasta mountain on the tray in front of him. Luckily I'd been too 'off' to eat breakfast so I was very helpful indeed.

'Lemony, I need you to do something for me.'

'Go away and stay away?'

'Quite the opposite, I need you to return to the cottage and look around, then report back. The crew and actors and extras will all be here again tomorrow and we might not get another chance. Bring Paul and Ro with you to be safe.'

I agreed, grateful to be able to do something helpful other than stuff my face with linguini. I'm now sitting in the large sitting room writing this, waiting for Paul to finish whatever he's up to so we can come up with a strategy together, and encouraging Ro not to call Bob, but to face her movie-world withdrawal head-on. Have to go fetch crisps to give her something to do other than stare at her silent walkie talkie.

LATER

We did it! I honestly thought we were wasting our time, but it was there! We ran straight from the cottage up to Stephen's room and he confirmed that the drawing we found was of the necklace. OK, so we didn't find the necklace itself, but it proves we are one step closer. With Ro on board we took a far more practical approach than just wading in with nothing but huge hope and a nervousness around shelves, instead we removed everything from the cottage and stacked it neatly outside, under a plastic sheet in case it rained before we put the stuff back.

We've all seen too many detective shows and were wearing such serious and knowing faces that anyone watching us would think Stephen had lost an arm in there and we'd been sent to fetch it. The empty cottage seemed properly empty as we didn't find anything treasure-shaped at all, no matter how much tugging of hooks and tapping of walls we did. We were just about to move the stuff back in and admit defeat when I thought that, if we were guessing with any kind of half-functioning minds, the necklace would have been buried beneath the ground. It would have been *under* the boulder so it would've had to have been below the floor not around the walls, window sills or fireplace.

Ro jumped all over this idea and wanted to call Bob to see what the chances were of lucking into some heavy floor-breaking machinery. In the end the demolition squad wasn't needed, as Paul noticed that not all the flagstones making up the floor were the same. One was slightly more battered looking, which made us think that maybe it might have had a more exciting life than the other flagstones. Sure enough, with the famous shelf for leverage we managed to lift it and underneath we found a roll of tough fabric with the sketch inside.

Well, at that stage we only knew it was a roll of fabric as I insisted we wait until getting to Stephen's room before looking inside, after all it wasn't *his* fault he was doing the wounded soldier bit while we all got to rove about like untamed detectives. Ro and Paul have started saying, 'It was the *shelf's* fault. *Bad shelf!*' every time they see me looking guilty and angst-ridden over the whole thing.

He'd been napping when we bounded in, but it would have taken a hard-of-hearing narwhal to sleep through our frenzy. Once Stephen had compared the drawing to that in one of the books and confirmed it as the one we wanted, we suddenly realised that it didn't bring us any closer to the *actual* necklace.

When trails go cold most wild trackers will spend hours sniffing around for a tiny clue to get them back on the scent again. However, we four Grangers decided we'd done enough for the day and played Scrabble. This was an historic event because for the first time in seven years I lost! Not to Stephen (although we were within two points of each other most of the time), but to Paul who is still insisting that 'dogsbreath' is one word and not two. We asked Professor Brown to adjudicate, but all we got was a ten-minute seminar on the nature of evolving language.

I was feeling a bit ropey after that so although it's

only five I'm in bed already and I think I'll sleep now. Miss Higgins wants to call the doctor for me again, but I'm sure I just need time to rest.

The crew is coming back tomorrow, which is perfect timing as I'm starting to miss them again. Ro agrees that our room is a little lonely without Lorna and Alice arguing over which of them is the best dancer and who has the best 'surprised face' and bonding over fashions it will take them a decade to afford.

Not feeling well AT ALL.

DAY TWENTY-THREE

It was like waking up in a church. Lorna, Alice, Amber, Bonnie and Hanna were all sitting on the other beds whispering so loudly it was really talking with a lot of breathing behind it, and telling each other to 'shhh' or they'd wake me. I told them it was too late for that and suddenly had a crowd of concerned faces around me. Apparently the story of the 'cottage accident' travelled around the place faster than it took for the catering truck to run out of pancakes. In their version of it poor, brave Lemony is regaining the use of her addled mind (while also in the throes of double pneumonia), while tragic Stephen's skull is hanging on by a thin piece of string. No matter how many times I told them I was fine and that I was up and about all day yesterday they wouldn't let me out of bed. Full-force caring. I feel sorry for the world if any of them go into medicine after school, they'd end up being the kind of surgeons who would amputate your stomach if it rumbled.

Miss Higgins called in and said that the extras wouldn't be needed for a couple of hours so the girls set up camp around my bed. I must admit it was lovely to be the centre of attention, even if it did involve listening to a *lot* of stories read from magazines and a running commentary from Amber on everyone who passed by down below outside the window. Paul knocked on the door, but didn't come in, leaving a note for me instead. I could tell from the handwriting that it was from Stephen, and as I didn't want any of them to get the wrong idea I laughed knowingly and pretended it was from Paul himself. I said he couldn't go ten minutes without needing to be obnoxious to me.

I shoved the unread piece of paper under the pillow and couldn't retrieve it for another hour. Finally my ladies-in-waiting were convinced that my demise was several years off as long as I avoided the coffee from catering, and I headed off to shower, managing to sneak the note away.

It read:

Dear Miss Smith,

Word has reached the castle that your health has waned overnight. Please send news forthwith as to the state of aforementioned health, as the success of the campaign depends upon it.

Your thoughtful gift of your brother Paul will prove useful in delivering this missive. He really is a most interesting and engaging servant, the first I have ever had to pay in bourbon creams.

Faithfully yours,

Sir Stephen Brown. (I promoted myself in your absence).

It made me laugh, but then I felt angry at the thought that the only reason he was asking about how I was doing was because he wanted me to help solve the mystery. I know this is a bit rich considering the damage I did to him recently, but I thought we were friends now. Maybe he's just using me as someone who can run around for him.

It's all a bit confusing.

I missed breakfast on the bus and have been eating so much rubbish recently that I asked Miss Higgins would she mind making me a vegetable stir-fry. I felt better after eating something good and have decided to eat fruit instead of biscuits today. Ro is back on form since Lizzy also made her a runner for the director on top of the few things she is still doing for Bob.

I actually caught her saying, 'Ten four on Julian's jacket. On the move from trailer to director's chair!'

I was so relieved to see Stephen on set in the ballroom wearing his soldier's uniform. The bandage was gone and Dipti had put make-up over the bruising, and the stitches and swelling were only visible close-up.

Perhaps because we'd had a few days off from filming, we had the BEST fun of any day since it started. During an endless wait for lighting, Lorna and Alice were teaching everyone how to tap dance on the wooden floor and soon most of the other extras and some of the crew joined in with the little routine. Most people were surprised that Lorna can tap, but I know her mum sent her for lessons in an optimistic attempt to make her more ladylike as ballet class would have been ridiculous under the circumstances. Ed the choreographer was the only one who wasn't too happy as he wanted us to be practising our old-fashioned dancing, quadrilles or whatever they're called. I caught Stephen sitting down a lot and having to get his strength back, so I sat with him while the others started into Hanna's hip-hop routine, and asked him what he thought we should do next, find the necklace or solve the break-ins.

'Find the necklace,' he spoke softly and leaned in so that no one would overhear, 'That way we can set a trap to catch the people who are after it.'

We spent ages sitting on one of the formal chaise longues, which the props department had put around the edges of the room, but couldn't talk about the necklace any more because Sophie came and sat with us. Given that there is no one her age she gets bored easily and feels she has to try really hard to fit in and Stephen was so good with her, telling her stories about kings and queens and showing her how to multiply huge numbers in her head. I couldn't help noticing how good he looked in his soldier's dress uniform, especially with his stitched-up head adding to the authenticity. (It's the *shelf's* fault. *Bad* shelf!)

Just as we got up to take our places for the next scene he asked me, 'How are you feeling?'

But I didn't get a chance to reply as Lizzie rushed me away to be in a group with some others. I caught sight of myself in a large mirror and didn't know who it was for a moment. Dipti and Wendy and the contact lens lady have worked some kind of miracle. I know looks don't matter, but under that special lighting I looked amazing, maybe even beautiful. Pity I don't have a makeover team and a spotlight to follow me through my real life!

Once we wrapped in the early evening I decided to write a note back to Stephen, just for the laugh. It said:

Dear Sir Stephen,

Your uniform buttons looked remarkably shiny today, as did my nose I fear. This was due to the mild cold that has settled upon me following one or two inadvisable outdoor excursions over the past two days and a slight fraying of the nerves.

If this were not trying enough, I cannot imagine how the campaign might proceed from this point onward. I seem to have left my brain behind at the scene of the accident. If you see it, do not approach for it can be a ferocious and troubling thing.

Yours ,

*Lady Lemony. (Now that you are also landed gentry I may
reveal my true identity.)*

I slipped it into his pocket as we went into the sitting
room to join the rest of the Grangers for one of Miss
Higgins' buffet dinners. He smiled at this, which
made me feel better than I have for days.

DAY TWENTY-FOUR

Ro and Paul have been gathering info. She's been talking to the security guards who say that it's obvious that the break-ins were done by two people who are probably working on the film, at least part time. Paul has been flirting with every woman under the age of a hundred and saying he is trying to find out if any of them have encountered anything strange. I think he means apart from himself.

The blonde woman hasn't been around since that day she was on the dining-bus, but it could be that she's part of a larger gang. It seems that Stephen is staying in bed today and I really wish he was here. This may be borderline insane, but I find it really exciting not knowing what he is going to say or do next. Like when I was putting on my costume shoes this morning and found this letter slipped inside one of them.

My Dear Lady Lemony,

May I be the first to offer reassurances that your nose was not nearly as shiny as the buttons of my coat, although most certainly it seemed to be a similar shade of red. Ever at your bidding I dispatched myself to the scene of my near-decapitation and believed at first that I had found your missing brain. Alas, on further examination it turned out to be an old deflated football. Should you deem this to be a suitable replacement I shall be honoured to convey it to you post-haste.

Yours ever gallantly,

Sir Stephen.

He really is funny, I think he just doesn't bother to barge his way into the limelight and insist on an audience the way Paul and Alex do. Now I am really paranoid that my nose might be red so I'm going to check in with make-up.

LATER

When I got to the hair and make-up room Dipti started laughing and said that she'd been told to expect me and that she was to tell me that my nose is beautiful and just the right colour. Then the rest of me went red as I blushed massively and rushed off to write a note in return. I knew the library would be quiet and was surprised to see Stephen run away from there as he was supposed to be in bed. He sailed right past me without saying hello and I presumed he'd found some evidence, but he hurried off too fast and I couldn't find him after that. Paul just checked his room, and Ro had half the crew on the walkie-talkies looking out for him, but he seems to have just vanished completely. I haven't felt much like writing to him; I just want to talk to him.

MUCH LATER

We didn't get any further in solving the mystery as Stephen got back while we were all eating dinner on the dining-buses (we wrapped really late) and went straight to bed. It's crazy-late.

DAY
TWENTY-FIVE

OK, something weird is going on. I mean *besides* the fact that we are wandering around in empire-line costumes with a full film crew and investigating break-ins and trying to find enchanted necklaces. Something very weird indeed.

NICK COLLINS is back working on the film and no one, not even Alex or Lizzie or Miss Higgins, knows why. Also this is the second day that Stephen has disappeared. I waited for him on the steps up to the attic rooms from eight this morning so he must have left even before that.

LATER

QUIZ

If you see a guy you have been day-dreaming about for two years and you find out he's not going out with Donna Henderson anymore because she has gone to her granny's, do you:

A) Trip romantically across the lawn in your fancy long dress to be swept up into his arms?

B) Stand at a slight distance being all fascinating for his benefit?

C) Not feel all that bothered and keep eating your fruit salad and talking to Mary-Ann from production?

And the answer, ladies and gentlemen, is ... (drum roll please) ... 'C'!! I hope this isn't evidence that my heart has shrivelled to the size of a dried prune through under-use. Nick was there at lunch, play-fighting with Gussy and Owen, and, I don't know, I think that if I had been fired I wouldn't be messing about and laughing so loudly during my first day back. He didn't even seem to realise how annoyed Lizzie looked or apologise to anyone or reassure them that he'll work properly this time.

Ro came over to me and Mary-Ann with the same face she wears when her mother makes her put the dogs in the garage, like she'd maim the first person to blink. Mary-Ann raised one eyebrow at me and sloped off to a safer part of the circus.

When Ro is in this rare mood the trick is not to talk first. Eventually she muttered through teeth *so* tightly clenched that her top and bottom jaw almost switched places, 'HE is Bob's new assistant.'

Followed by a two-minute silence during which I did nothing but keep holding my empty spoon and looking at her with an expression of slight concern, careful that it didn't spill over into one of pity.

'NICK,' she eventually continued, quietly, but with enough force to shoot rabbits. 'They have asked me to train *Nick* into being the new assistant location manager.'

'So what job will you be doing?'

'Julian's personal assistant.'

'Well, isn't that a better job for you? Helping out the director?' I was getting braver now.

'It's the *principle* of the thing.'

I have never been good at arguing principles so I just nodded.

'I'm not into him any more if that's any consolation,' I said.

It was only when it was out of my mouth that I fully realised it was true.

With that Ro and I sat grinning at each other for ages before going off to just run about the place laughing. One serious bright side is that the assistant location manager does quite a bit of clearing away of rubbish and I can't imagine that goes with Nick's image of himself. I wonder how he managed to make his way back onto the film though. This afternoon they only used about half the extras for a scene around the window in the ballroom so Lizzy said us Grangers could change back into our normal clothes and just hang out.

When Stephen hadn't reappeared by five I went wandering around the grounds. Eventually I found him sitting on the boulder, but as I made my way over he got up and walked away down another path. I know for a fact that I haven't physically or mentally tortured him in the last forty-eight hours so it's all a bit confusing. I now want to find out something more about the necklace mystery, then leave a note for him and maybe that way he'll come back from wherever his head's at.

LATER

Ro had kept the drawing of the necklace and the piece of fabric in her suitcase for safe-keeping.

Thinking it might inspire me, I took it out and just stared at the sketch and the fabric-roll for ages. Eventually I noticed that the fabric was synthetic, made from a modern fibre that wouldn't have been available until the last century. I went in search of Professor Brown to check my theory. That man knows EVERYTHING there is to know in life, he's a walking university all on his own.

I could hear him inside his office, but although I knocked quite loudly three times, he didn't answer. Eventually I turned the handle and opened the door slowly. His office looks more like a nest or a junkyard than a room. Hundreds of books stacked around the place on chairs, on the floor, everywhere except on the bookshelves, which are groaning under the weight of strange objects; stuffed animals, awards, small bits of clockwork, pipes, pieces of ancient pottery, and dozens of antique mechanical typewriters, which he collects. As usual Professor Brown was crouched over a sheaf of papers and didn't notice me until I was right beside his desk.

'Lemony, dear girl, is everything all right?'

'Yes, thank you. I just wanted to show you this. Would I be right in thinking it's not from the time The Grange was built.'

On seeing the roll of fabric he jumped up with glee and said, 'Oh, *you* found it did you?' and giggled away to himself for a while. He then cleared a mountain of sweaters and exam papers from a nearby chair and invited me to sit down while he explained something to me.

Apparently we were right in finding where the necklace had been hidden, a spot that had been known to the Professor since he had done the detective work himself as a boy. However, before the film crew arrived the Professor fetched the necklace from its hiding place in a small wooden box under the flagstone. He replaced it with the drawing, which he copied from the original onto a very old piece of paper, before wrapping it in a length of fabric which had just been lying around. He'd thought that any thieves might find the drawing and think that it was all there was to be had.

'So where is the necklace now?' I hoped he'd be able to produce it from a safe lurking beneath the stuffed armadillo or something.

'Do you know, my dear, I put it down somewhere and now can't for the life of me remember where that was. I'm sure it will turn up safely, thieves rarely see things that are unhidden. You will let me know if you come across it won't you? I'm presuming it's still around as the old place is still standing!'

And with that he laughed his cute little laugh and went back to what he'd been working on when I came in.

I was amazed! My own folks can be a bit dusty in the head especially when they are writing an academic paper or when it's near exam time, but Stephen's dad is a real-life, proper eccentric. I ran and told Ro that we *had* to have a meeting at midnight in the library and to make sure Paul and Stephen were there.

LATER STILL

I'm in the girls' bathroom now, having just got back from the meeting. I was the last to get to the library and found Stephen, Ro and Paul all sitting in the armchairs, laughing about something that had happened where a props guy was found asleep in one of the luxury cars for the actors, but not until the actor almost sat on him.

I noticed that Stephen went completely silent when I walked in and wouldn't look at me. I suppose he's had time to get angry about how I caused the accident, because I can't think of anything else I might have said or done wrong since. It's strange how we were getting on so well until yesterday. Maybe he's just moody like Lorna can be.

After I told them about my conversation with the Professor, they couldn't take it in and asked me to say it again. Stephen put his head in his hands.

'I'm so sorry,' he said. 'My father is a strange one. It's just that he's so brilliant that he doesn't connect well with the real world somehow. My mother used to be his go-between and interpreter, but in the six years since she died he's got more and more withdrawn.'

We reassured Stephen that we thought it was a stroke of genius on his dad's part to move the necklace and that we'd find it as soon as possible. He still wouldn't look at me, though, in fact, he almost seemed to flinch when I spoke to him.

Paul then had an idea. 'Look, we don't have the necklace, right?'

'Right,' we agreed to the glaringly obvious.

'So what if we *pretend* we have it, put word out on set that it's in a box in here or something and then we lie in wait and trap the people who are looking to steal it.'

It sounded too simple, but after letting it sink in for

a minute or two we all agreed that we had nothing to lose. The best way to make sure everyone knows is to tell Amber, who must have been a parrot or a newspaper in a former life.

The plan is that we are going to let the news filter through and then leave it until the night after next before lying in wait. There's no way they could plan a break-in with only a few hours notice. Just in case, Paul is going to sleep in the library tomorrow night. Stephen wanted to take first watch, but the rest of us agreed that it would be best if he got himself fully mended first. We decided not to let any of the others know what's been going on, especially not Alex as he'd tell his dad and then we wouldn't be able to lay the trap.

I must start bringing a pillow in here as the tiled floor is really cold.

DAY TWENTY-SIX

They were shooting with just the actors this morning and afternoon and Miss Higgins said they didn't need us until the evening. After a great deal of aimless wandering, I found Paul and Stephen outside sitting on the large rock near the orchard. When Stephen jumped up to leave, as he's been doing of late, Paul said to stay in case I might have news. I feel really sad that he's avoiding me, but I know I deserve it for what I've done to him over the past couple of weeks. But I do wonder why he was so nice to me for a while, was that just so I'd feel worse now? If so, then it's working.

Anyway, I'd had what I thought was a stroke of mini-genius. If the film is partly based on the story of the necklace then what if the necklace that Antonia is wearing in the early scenes has been switched for the original? None of us could remember what the one she'd been wearing looked like, but it was obvious who's connected enough with the props department to find out.

'I'll ask her!' Paul was up like a shot and ran off to find Ro.

That left me and Stephen alone together and I took a deep breath before asking,

'Stephen have I done anything wrong? It seems as if you've been avoiding me for the past few days.'

He looked at me as if he couldn't work out what I was saying and eventually replied, 'Lemony, you have loads of friends, you don't need me pretending to be one of them.'

And off he walked again. I am completely miserable. I know I wasn't nice to him but I don't feel I deserve this, I *really* don't.

The next time I saw him was after dinner when we were back in costume in the ballroom. In this scene I was sitting with Hanna and Sophie and he was with

Alex and Gussy so we didn't get to talk. We kept going for take after take and at midnight catering brought in Chinese food and pizzas to the ballroom for everyone. To ensure we didn't spill anything while eating off our laps Wendy made us all wear black garbage bags over our costumes with holes cut for head and arms. We looked hilarious.

Everyone's energy sagged *massively* after midnight and I was praying for someone to start handing out the call sheets (bits of paper with the details about who is doing what and when for the next day) as that usually meant we were about to finish. I was exhausted. Mid-yawn Julian came over to me and I presumed he was going to tell me I was doing something wrong or to sit up straighter. Instead he asked me if I had ever acted before! The question was *so* unexpected and what little focus I could muster had been absorbed into the pizza, so I didn't think and just went, 'Not unless you count the time I pretended I actually liked my Dad's new orange car.'

He laughed and said, 'Well, there's a scene coming up tomorrow with two very short lines and I have it on good authority that you are something of an actress. Would you like to give it a go?'

'Love to,' I said, almost passing out with the shock.

I figured Ro must have had a sneaky hand in it, but she was as surprised and delighted with the news as Paul and the others were. Ro reckons that Danny and Driggers from the props department will be able to show her the necklace in two days time as it's being worn by Antonia until then and she's in costume first thing every day.

I didn't tell her about what Stephen said. It feels bad not to be able to share my good news with him.

Way, way, way, way, waaaayyyy past bedtime now.

DAY TWENTY-SEVEN

We had the morning off and I mostly slept, then first thing this afternoon Miss Higgins sent me over to Lizzy. She then packed me off to meet Mr Flynn, the dialogue and accent coach, who is one of only a handful of people on set I haven't talked to before, to 'run my lines'. They're not really full lines, just 'No Sir, I did not', and 'That way, my Lord', but you'd be amazed how many thousands of ways there are to say them. After ten minutes working with Mr Flynn I asked him would they not just get someone else to do it, like Alice who's a natural at being dramatic, but he said I'll be *wonderful*. My *stomach* doesn't feel so wonderful and I'm sitting alone in a trailer (which I get for the day seeing as I'm classed as an actor not an extra) and wishing Ro or Stephen were here to say things to make me feel like less of a fake.

Earlier this afternoon Ro brought me over a form I needed to sign to get paid for today and get a credit, and she then had to cycle over to our house to get Mum or Dad to sign it too, which is why she's been gone for a while.

Paul went with her to show her the way although she has only been there nearly every day since nursery school! He is *so obvious* that it hurts to see him.

Wendy and Dipti keep dropping round and are all proud of me and making sure I keep looking my best. All I can think of is that Antonia will be wearing the necklace and I'll get to see it close up.

It's funny how sometimes you end up living a reality before you even know it. Like the time Mum and Dad made me learn the violin for eight years longer than necessary. In the beginning I thought it would simply involve a lifetime of painful scratching and scraping, sounding like tuneless kittens, but suddenly without any effort bigger than showing up I suddenly found I could play quite well. I've just this minute realised that only a few weeks ago Ro and I were doing the thing from that *Game of Life* book and I decided to test it and ask to be a film star. And now, without even trying or doing anything except reacting to whatever came my way, and here I am: script in hand, Dipti from hair and make-up fussing over me, about to walk out on set to deliver my lines. This is incredible!!!

Right! I'm now going to ask for what I *really* want. That chinchilla would still be good, the ability to speak another language, to have Stephen be my friend again, to do a good job with this scene in about ten minutes ...

Ten minutes? Did Lizzie just say ten minutes? NERVES! Nerves are kicking in like mad old mules, I want this to be OVER and done with!

LATER

Did it!

I got through the scene and found it far easier to say the lines when the actors were there speaking too. We had to do it about ten times, and each time that something didn't go exactly right it had NOTHING to do with me. Either someone else fluffed their line or a plane flew overhead, or the boom got in shot, or Julian changed his mind about something. With all the commotion I almost forgot to check out the necklace around Antonia's neck, but it was obvious from first glance that it was a fake and only slightly like the drawing in the book. All the same I asked her if it was heavy and she showed me that is was made of plastic and quite light. So much for *that* big idea.

I did make use of the moment to ask if she'd heard that the original was kept in the Grange library. She was interested to hear that, but one of the other actors seemed overly-interested, almost twitchy at the subject. He asked me loads of questions such as how I knew about the necklace, and where exactly was it kept, and had I seen it. I don't know the actor's name but his character is called Mr Rollins and Ro will be able to find out his real name from the call sheet.

Lorna, Alice, Hanna, Sophie, Amber, Bonnie, Gussy, Owen and Alex as well as loads of the other regular extras and my crew friends like Bob and Wendy, were all waiting for me at the side and rushed over to tell me what a great job I did. Julian even let me watch the playback and I did look good, or at least I didn't stick out like a piece of green at a red fest. In fact I totally blended in as if I belonged just as much as the others. I also noticed that Antonia and the other lead actress are both taller than I am.

Nick passed by and said, 'Famous now are we, taller twin?'

I just sighed. How can I have wasted such creative daydreams on a person so small inside?

Stephen was standing near the catering truck beside the salad buffet table, which hadn't yet been cleared away. Feeling braver now that I had done the scene I walked right over. He congratulated me on the scene, but looked so uncomfortable that I couldn't stand it a moment longer. I knew I was making a complete idiot of myself but I didn't care.

'Stephen, I, um … OK! I really miss you. I miss our talks together, our adventures, the letters … and I just … I'd like us to be friends again. Or friends in the first place if you believe we weren't before. I would very much like that. If it's possible that you might want to be my friend …'

Then I amazed myself by adding, '… or more'.

Just then Gussy and Alex arrived at the table, being loudly disappointed that it was salad and not dessert. So instead of answering me with even a simple 'yes' or 'we'll see' or 'no way', Stephen just picked up a bowl of stuffed olives and said, 'Olive?' and then out of nowhere loads of people came over and crowded around the food, and before I knew it he was gone. RECAP: I offered him myself and he offered me an olive. Typical me, typical me!

Then, like a rain storm right after your picnic has been eaten by ants, Ro walked right over and said, 'Seeing as you are in such a good mood after your brilliant acting...' (although by then I was way down thanks to the olives) '... I just thought you should know that me and your brother ... Paul ...'

'Yes, I know his name.'

'Er, we sort of kissed.'

'What's a "sort of" kiss?'

'OK, we kissed.'

I couldn't be angry with her so I smiled and said, 'There's a three-litre bottle of industrial-strength disinfectant in the utility room, gargle with that and you'll be fine.'

Then she surprised me by saying, 'I've had a thing for him for as long as you liked Nick. I just never said because I didn't think he'd ever see me as anything other than his little sister's friend.'

'Is that why you never went out with anyone for longer than a fortnight?'

'I tried, but none of them were a patch on him. Are you OK with this? After all, first-and-foremost I'm your best friend and that will never change. Except you probably won't be so pushy for details on this one.'

That made me laugh.

'Strange girl. Now run along and tell him that I didn't faint or scream at the news.'

And she did. And I think I'm fine with it.

The word for the day is 'resigned'. I refuse to get upset, after all, no doubt more things will be along for me to worry over and I have to pace myself.

DAY TWENTY-
EIGHT

We were right about the thieves not making a move last night. Paul slept right across the doorway just in case, and was nearly knocked out by Miss Higgins when she came to find out where he'd got to in the morning. Paul concocted a story about Gussy snoring and Alex singing in his sleep to explain his presence there.

Julian has drafted me into another scene. For this one I'm what's called a 'special extra', there's only me sitting with Antonia and the Mr Rollins actor, whose name I neglected to find out from Ro. The upshot of this sudden promotion is that I've been on set in the rose garden all day. I have no idea why anyone would want to be an actor unless every other job in the universe was taken, except for maybe jobs like having to clip someone's toenails for a living or carry pianos and kitchen sinks up desolate mountains on your back. It seems that everyone else on set is having a better time than the actors. Dipti gets to be creative and chat with people all day, Julian is constantly having to think up new ideas, the first and second ADs are like generals in the military, Ro is making an art out of being a personal assistant, the catering staff get to feel good about getting everyone fed with good food on time, and even as an ordinary extra you can chill out more as no one really notices you unless you are goofing around like Nick used to.

Which reminds me, I saw Nick and Stephen around the place both picking up rubbish and moving parking bollards. I know that's part of Nick's job, but it doesn't make sense why Stephen would be helping him. Am I living in some weird alternate universe where a geek would choose to be friends with a loud-mouth jock instead of with another geek like me? Strange and spooky stuff.

Dipti just told me that this green ribbon in my hair makes my eyes look really green, and that I must wear this colour more often. Wendy told me I can keep the hair-ornament from the lilac costume as a souvenir, but not to tell anyone as it really should go back at the end of shooting. I'm all fancied up in yet another stunning dress, this one a deep peacock blue with black silk shoes (teamed with the old anorak and woolly hat between takes). I was moaning about the fact that the weather had been so bad, but Antonia told me stories about bubbling away under the Saharan sun during one movie she starred in and I now feel quite grateful for the chill. I can't believe that by this time next week it will all be over.

Part of me feels happy that Julian has given me this opportunity and part of me envies the fun I can see Amber and Alice and the girls having on the bus, and the conversations between Ro and Paul, which are probably about our next plan of action. I have even lost my grip on the biscuit traffic as I was on set when Caro brought them out to the table. Unless things improve I might find myself having to beg for a simple digestive.

LATER

I was inside my trailer writing when the funniest thing happened. A lighting man who I have seen quite often, but haven't ever spoken to, knocked on the door and told me he had a message. He said I was to 'meet Sir Stephen at the Augean Stables as soon as possible', and added that he hoped it made sense to me because it didn't to him. There are no actual stables at The Grange, so I guessed – because in Greek mythology the Augean Stables were full of cattle manure that Hercules had to clear out – that it must mean the cottage (which is also kind of bunged up with all other kinds of untidiness).

I had to dodge Lizzy, but managed to sneak into the cottage without being seen. Stephen was standing waiting.

He gave me a reluctant-looking smile, and said,

'Wow, Lemony, only you could have worked out that message. I couldn't come to your trailer because I'm finding it hard to dodge Nick and we can't risk being overheard.'

'I don't have long, they could need me on set any moment.'

Stephen still seemed sort of distant, but at least he was talking to me.

'OK, here it is,' he said quickly, 'I've figured out why people might be looking for the necklace. I escaped for long enough this morning to go through some things in my father's office, sorting out papers and oddments in the hope that the necklace might be lodged between a thesaurus and a six-month old sandwich—'

Just then we heard Lizzy and Ro in the distance shouting, 'Lemony!' so we had to push the speed button.

'In short, I found a blackmail letter to my father saying that they would steal the necklace and The Grange would fall to the ground, *unless* he deposited this huge amount of money in a Swiss bank account.'

'Right, two questions,' (by now we could hear them send Bonnie up to the attic room to look for me). 'One, how would your Dad get that kind of money on a lecturer's salary? Two, why didn't your Dad take the note to the police?'

By now we were both talking as fast as machine guns.

'One, a little more searching and I discovered a solicitor's letter about an inheritance from two years ago from an aunt of my mother's. Two, you know what he's like, it would have been gone from his mind the moment a new theory for the preservation of ceramic artifacts arrived in.'

Just then Ro opened the cottage door, rolled her eyes and dragged me away telling her walkie-talkie, 'Lemony on the move.' Stephen smiled at me and then seemed to catch himself and frowned and looked away quickly just as I disappeared back outside.

Although we are now on another break Miss Higgins and Lizzy insist I stay right here in the trailer. I also have to say four more words in the next scene – 'Oh yes, quite well', when someone asks if we are well and Antonia's character is too taken aback to answer. I wish that instead I could be in the Professor's office hunting for the necklace or in the library working out the best place to hide tonight. Mr Flynn is on his way to make me say my line two million times. Being a film star sucks.

STILL LATER

Finally we wrapped around nine pm. Stephen was helping Nick to guide the cars out and pick up rubbish and again that seemed odd. I can now get changed in my trailer and Wendy takes care of my costume. Giving her that additional work didn't feel good so I hung everything up carefully and left her a thank-you note, although I was absolutely straining to flee and plan the stake-out with the others.

All significant talk had to wait a while also, as Miss Higgins had the buffet for the Grangers ready in the kitchen. The eight of us were talking about everything that's happened in the last couple of weeks. I caught Stephen's eye and he seemed to be thinking what I was thinking about how the others, Gussy, Alex, Alice and Lorna, didn't know the half of what had been going on around here. Just as happened earlier he grinned at me, but then looked embarrassed and didn't glance my way again.

Already people are getting excited about the wrap party, the big final 'well done and goodbye' party they have when they finish shooting. It's scheduled for a week after we finish as the rest of the crew will be filming on the quayside for a few days after leaving here. Alice was getting frazzled and saying she couldn't *possibly* go because she has nothing good to wear, so Lorna suggested that all us girls go on a shopping trip and spend some of our wages on new outfits. Might be a plan. You could tell that all this banter was driving Stephen and Paul a bit nuts and they skipped off just before the cocoa arrived. Ro gave me the same, 'Stay!' look she gives the dogs and I got that it would look too obvious if we fled at the same time. I knocked back the scalding cocoa and did the fakest yawn to ever come from a so-called actor's mouth. I then announced that I'd take myself off upstairs, adding that I thought we were *all* looking a bit tired.

Miss Higgins was pleased that I was going to bed early, and told Lorna that she should follow my example. If poor Miss Higgins had *any* idea....

DAY TWENTY-NINE

Ro and I stayed fully dressed under the covers and crept out soon after Lorna stopped talking about how much she doesn't fancy Alex (enough of a favourite theme to cause doubt) and Alice finally stopped fretting about what she'd wear to the wrap party. I counted to sixty in my head and knew that neither of them could be silent for a whole minute if still awake.

Paul and Stephen were already in the library and had set up three kinds of camp. One was a blanket under the large writing desk. The desk was covered as always with a table-cloth that reached the ground so Ro and I could happily hide in there without being seen. Stephen was to be behind the curtain beside the giant urn on a bar stool brought in from the billiards room, and insisted he'd be happier sitting up all night than lying down. Paul decided to camp out below the stairs in case they planned to enter or exit that way, and had some cushions hidden in the space under there.

Ro ordered me to sleep for the first hour saying she'd wake me if anything happened. In the end she decided to let me sleep on and it was three-and-a-half hours later when she shook me awake with her hand over my mouth in case I spoke.

I got it! There were others in the library!

My heart began to beat even faster than that time I had to play 'We Are Happy Horses, Happy, Happy Horses' at the violin recital at the age of eight and hadn't practised.

The thieves seemed to be searching for the necklace in utter silence, only the slight sounds of rubber soles on wood and carpet gave them away. I realised that my leg was tingling and going numb and didn't want that to happen in case we had to chase the intruders anytime soon. As carefully as possible I shifted my weight, but my foot caught the edge of the table cloth and moved it a couple of inches – enough to dislodge a pen from the desktop which rolled to the ground, the slight sound breaking through the night. At that same moment Stephen stepped out from behind the curtain and confronted whoever was there. I could hear them rushing for the door as Ro and I scrambled out from our burrow. Ro managed to grab the ankles of one of them who crashed down onto the rug, while Stephen and I grabbed at the other person just as a sleepy-eyed Paul rushed in the door. He locked the door behind himself and Stephen yelled at me to secure the windows.

I could clearly see that it was the blonde lady from that night in the courtyard and the actor who played Mr Rollins. They immediately started to try to talk their way out of it, acting all friendly and surprised, saying they were afraid that someone was going to try and steal the necklace so they came in to protect it. Next they said that The Professor told them they could use the library whenever they wanted. Then they tried offering us money. Not often finding ourselves in this position of capturing thieves and never having discussed this part of the plan, we honestly didn't know what to do next so we let them talk on for a couple of minutes until there was a heavy knocking at the library door and the night-time security guards from the set appeared along with The Professor.

It seems he'd been working late in his office, heard the noise and called the police. Quite a surprising move for The Professor who you would expect to wander in, shuffle about looking for a book before offering the thieves a mint and leaving again.

It only took a few minutes for the police to arrive and arrest them, all done without waking anyone else in the house. The taking of statements in the library took an hour longer, but eventually it was just us and the Professor sitting in the large leather armchairs, with Ro and Paul cross-legged on the sheepskin rug in front of the fireplace.

The first thing Ro said was, 'Good thing the Mr Rollins character isn't needed for any more scenes,' and we all laughed at how much of a film-pro she'd become.

I didn't manage to get back to sleep, unlike Ro who hadn't slept at all and was out for the count. Once I saw it was five-thirty and the sun was coming up I decided to get showered and dressed for the day and go outside. Something told me that Stephen would be up too, and sure enough I found him sitting on his rock. For a while we sat there in silence looking at all the colours growing brighter as the sun inched higher. Finally Stephen spoke. I guessed he wasn't so angry with me any more.

'You know, Lemony, I'm really annoyed with my father. I thought all along that we were just financially scraping by because it takes so many people to keep such a large house going. I thought the reason he'd chosen to let the film be shot here was to pay some bills with the rental fee, and all the time he's had this enormous inheritance.'

Most would think that finding out you had a wealthy parent might be cause for celebration, but I understood his anger.

'Is this about you having to work night and day to keep your scholarship?'

'Perhaps,' he acknowledged.

'Well it seems to me that your dad played a blinder on that one. Stephen, you are more knowledgeable on more subjects than any teenager I've ever met, and you have better study habits than anyone else in your school. If you hadn't had to work so hard I bet you'd have been bored with the partying soon enough.'

'True,' he visibly warmed to the idea, 'and as things are now I should be able to choose to go to any university in the world. Maybe he *did* know what he was doing.'

'I think there's more to your dad than any of us could guess at.'

If anyone had told me a month ago that I would want Nick Collins to go away so I could keep talking with Stephen Brown I would have set them up with some kind of specialist appointment. But it happened just then when Nick walked across to the orchard and said, 'Sorry to butt in on the geek convention, but we have work to do before Bob gets here.'

'You mean *you* have work to do,' I corrected.

'Well, Stevey here is responsible for making sure my work is up to the production department's exacting high standards and the only way that's going to happen is if he does it with me.'

'Or *for* you,' Stephen muttered.

It doesn't make sense, why would Stephen be in charge of whether or not Nick does a good job? That would be like Sophie being in charge of whether *I* know my lines. And they were off, leaving me here to write this. Better go get some breakfast and reassure

Miss Higgins I'm alive.

LATER

Today has been another great day on set and I managed to stop yawning for long enough to say my line. No one seems to have heard about the actor and the blonde woman being arrested and I'd say that it might stay that way. I can't help wondering what happened to the necklace, though.

STILL LATER

If I ever do win an Oscar it will only be when they start giving them out for being the biggest IDIOT in the world!

It now *all* makes sense, why Stephen was being friendly to me and then being all distant. I have never wished so much that I could turn back time, or transform into someone else entirely, or disappear, or get to live on a different planet. Any of those, I'd happily take *any* of those.

I was sitting with Alice, reassuring her that no one thinks she's over-emotional and handing her the twenty-seventh Kleenex of the hour, when Owen came over to where we were sitting on these chairs in the courtyard and suddenly she was more interested in hearing *him* say that she's perfect as she is. Which is fair enough. I went in the side door that most of the film people don't know about, and saw Stephen on the furthest couch in the darkened empty sitting room and it seemed the perfect opportunity to find out what the deal was with Nick.

Fearing that we'd be interrupted as usual I just launched straight in.

'Stephen, I know you wouldn't keep a secret from me. Not now after we have proven ourselves to be master co-investigators and defenders of justice. Tell me, why are you saving Nick Collins from getting fired again?'

He seemed too tired to fight me on this one.

'Because I got him his job back, and promised Julian and Mary-Ann that I'd be personally responsible for Nick carrying out his duties correctly.'

'But why would you do a thing like that? I mean, you've never even been friends with Nick!'

'Because I found your shopping list.'

That one had me *completely* floored.

'What do you mean you found my shopping list? I don't even have a shopping list.'

And then he produced a page from his back

pocket, a sheet that seemed to be from this journal, and handed it to me to read.

I almost sank to the floor with shame. It was the wish-list I'd written before we even got here. The one where I said I wanted to be a film star and Nick's girlfriend and for Stephen to keep away from me and stop thinking we could ever be friends. No *wonder* he's been avoiding me!

'Oh my God, Stephen, I wrote this *ages* ago, right after Mum and Dad's party.'

'I found it in the library under a chair when I was looking for the necklace. I presumed you'd written it that day.'

I realised it must have fallen out of the back of this when I threw it under the chair to run out to the cottage in the rain. Stephen looked *so* hurt as he showed it to me, and it made me feel *way* beyond awful.

'No! I ... Oh my God! It isn't anything I want *now*, and I don't even know if I really did then. I have *no* idea what I can say to make this right. I am *so* sorry. I say that a lot don't I? I know I've blown my last chance with you a long time ago, but if you wouldn't mind I'd still like to know what this has to do with helping Nick.'

He explained that he decided that if I really wanted to be Nick's girlfriend then he'd be a good friend and make that happen. It turns out that he was also the one to have a word with Julian and ask him if there were any lines or special extra parts coming up for a girl. I still can't believe it. I was so awful to him and here he was doing everything to make my dreams come true. Even by staying away from me. I felt so dreadful that before I could say another word to him I ran off to the girls' bathroom and I've been here writing and crying for the past two hours. A little while ago a note came under the door. It read:

Dear Lady Lemony,

Please, please don't cry any more.

Yours as always,

Sir Stephen.

Which of course made me feel a million times worse and cry even harder. How is it I keep messing everything up so badly? The worst of it is that now I'm terrified that Stephen will end up bringing Amber or Bonnie to the wrap party.

I really need sleep. I really need lots of things. I can't help thinking what a shame it is that we didn't replace my brain with that deflated football while we had the chance.

DAY THIRTY

Nick is too afraid of not being invited to the wrap party to mess up, so he had to do a full day's work all by himself today. It seems that Bob kept him busy because tomorrow is the big move to the quayside.

It was really sad today, kind of like last day at science camp, swapping of contact details, photos, and promises to stay in touch. Antonia signed a lovely photo of the two of us, Julian said I was the best novice he'd ever worked with, and Caro gave me a box of biscuits and a huge hug. Ro gets to work with them next week too, so I'm sure I'll hear loads of news.

It's too late to write much more as we had a party

in the kitchens for us Grangers, the other teenage extras and our favourite friends from set, Wendy, Lizzie, Dipti, Bob, John, Caro and some of the older extras. Even The Professor came down to join us and when Hanna showed him how to dance I thought Stephen and Miss Higgins would never stop laughing. This has been the best summer of my life, even taking into account all the dreadful ways I've been messing up.

DAY
THIRTY-ONE

This morning in the dining room (the last time all us Grangers will be eating breakfast together) there was a note with my name on slipped under my cup. It read:

Dear Lady Lemony,

Given the recent news of your reported loss of interest in Mr Nicholas of Collins, I hereby wish to offer my services as companion 'and more' and escort you to the ball.

Kindly reply in all haste.

Yours ever hopefully,

Sir Stephen of Great Patience.

I quickly penned a reply and slid it across the table to him, glad that everyone else was too absorbed in their own conversations to notice.

Dear Sir Stephen,

I WOULD <u>LOVE</u> TO GO TO THE WRAP PARTY WITH YOU!!!

Yours, really yours,

Lady Lemony of the Thousand Mistakes.

The guys were all called away after that to help with moving the props furniture from the ballroom, and after lounging around over endless cups of tea Lorna, Alice and I decided to go back to our bedroom, plan our party outfits and start to pack.

I came across the hair-ornament that Wendy let me keep with the lilac piece of ribbon and feather that she'd added, and thought that if I took those off it would be wearable just with the metal and fake-jewels part. That way I could wear it at the party with my hair done the way that Dipti taught me. Only when Alice said,

'You could wear it as a brooch too,' did I suddenly see what I was holding! I ripped away the feather and the ribbon.

Alice often rushes from rooms with no prior warning so she probably thought some cute guy had arrived downstairs when I suddenly tore from the room in search of Stephen, Ro and Paul.

Luckily they were all together by then tidying the Professor's office, with the Professor himself reading by the window.

'LOOK!' was all I could manage to say.

'Could it...?' was all Stephen could ask.

We rushed over to the window-seat and put it in front of the Professor's gaze.

It took him a moment before he face lit up.

'Ah, yes. *There* it is,' was all he said. 'Now be sure and put it back where it belongs.'

He seemed more amazed at the way the four of us couldn't stop laughing than at the fact that we'd found the necklace. The chain had been wound in and around the spirals and hoops, in a way that was so artistic that it never occurred to me that it could possibly be a neck chain, and the place where it ended in three small loops made it so perfect for holding in your hair that I never thought it could be made for anything else. Wendy had bent it a bit but I straightened it out with one move and just stared at the diamonds and wondered how I hadn't noticed. It's strange how easy it is to miss the value of something that's right under your nose all the time.

We decided, as usual, to keep it to ourselves.

Wendy was still packing away the female extras' wardrobe when Ro and I wandered in as nonchalantly as we could. I asked if she might have a small wooden box, saying it was for a present for a friend and she came up with the box that the Professor later confirmed was the original. He must have left it in that bedroom before the film people arrived.

I know I'll see everyone again in a week, but it does feel odd to think it's all over.

Straight after dinner, with most of the trucks and film people moved on and plenty of Grangers still running about, I suddenly felt a little overwhelmed again. So, meeting Miss Higgins on the attic steps with an armful of books from the boys' bedroom I offered to return them to the library.

I put the books on the large writing desk, the one Ro and I had hidden under, promising myself I'd shelve them properly later. Right at that moment I simply felt like hiding away, and knew that every other corner of the house would be buzzing with chat about recent events. I also felt that the window nook would be an obvious place to look if anyone wanted to find me. So I took a cushion from one of the armchairs and crawled under the table, knowing that no one would see me if they came in. I sat hugging the cushion under the table for ages, I've no idea how long, just letting my brain catch up with itself, and letting the rest of me calm down. I took the necklace from the box in my pocket and placed it around my neck. There was nothing scary about it any more, it just felt like a beautiful, magical work of art that made me feel connected to the past.

Eventually someone walked in, but I was confident they'd be gone when they saw the place apparently empty. For a minute the person seemed to pace the room, then they stopped and all was silent. The next thing a hand lifted the edge of the tablecloth and someone appeared. It was Stephen, crawling under the table to join me, sitting close and looking at me as if I was suddenly new. It had been days since I saw him wearing anything other than his soldier's costume, and he seemed as worn out as I felt.

'Lemony, Lady Lemony,' he said softly, as he

settled himself in. 'My apologies for arriving uninvited to your secret hideaway like this, however I have something very important to share with you.'

I couldn't even speak to reply as he placed his hands on either side of my face and pulled me close and kissed me very gently. He then kissed me again and again.

Everything was just as I would wish it to be.

A minute later we heard Miss Higgins calling for Stephen so he escorted me to one of the armchairs and smiled as he handed me this journal and my pen before leaving me there. I can see the portrait of the woman of the necklace from here, and she seems to be smiling at me.

DAY THIRTY-TWO

Mum and Dad are at their symposium so the Professor invited us to stay on at the Grange (my guess is with some prodding from Stephen and Miss Higgins), and Ro's folks said she could stay for a couple more days too. The crew has a couple of days off today so Ro was able to be with us.

This morning we re-buried the diamond necklace under the flagstone in the cottage and then (carefully) messed the place up again to discourage future treasure-hunters.

Then the four of us spent hours wandering around

the grounds, talking over the small things that had happened to us separately and that the others hadn't heard about. Paul told us he'd been in the make-up room when this extra asked Dipti to make her look ten years younger and she'd give her a whole day's wages. Ro remembered the night she had to go around to the nearest neighbours of The Grange and ply them with chocolates to stop them from calling the police for noise disturbance during one of the late shoots. Stephen confessed that he loved the catering pancakes so much that one day he went back three times, the third time claiming it was for an extra who'd hurt his foot and was on the bus. I told them about how Driggers from props had a thing for Wendy, but that she couldn't stand him because he smokes. Paul spoke to Alex's dad one day and found out when the movie is due to be released next year ... On and on and on we went even after Miss Higgins called us in for dinner.

Tonight was the chess championship playing by 'Smith House Rules', where all moves must be completed within one minute and if you take someone's queen you can opt to switch sides with your opponent. Paul won, but we expected that.

DAY THIRTY-THREE

Today was our last day at The Grange. We mostly sat talking in the large sitting room and we finished off tidying the Professor's office, which now looks neat and respectable, but still like a treasure trove.

Dad came to collect us at ten this evening and we dropped Ro home. It feels really strange and empty to be back home. Paul and I just sat in the kitchen for ten minutes and it was like we were reminding each other of what was missing so we both told Mum and Dad a 'parent-friendly' version of what we've been up to and disappeared off to our rooms. I have that feeling that nothing in life is ever going to be as good as the last few weeks.

Only when Mum asked me what I wanted for my birthday did I realise that it's going to be on the same day as the wrap party. I said I didn't really want to celebrate my birthday this year.

ONE WEEK LATER

I never did discover where Stephen went to on those days when he disappeared. Then this morning I found out! He was over here talking with my parents and helping them choose my birthday presents. As I opened them at the breakfast table I was expecting to get things that were nice, but not what I *really* wanted, and was amazed (and confused) to open a package with a shallow plastic bowl inside.

'That's only part of it,' Mum explained. 'Look outside.'

There on the lawn was a big hutch and inside I

could see a pair of chinchillas hopping about. I filled the bowl with water and, still in my pyjamas, went out to give it to them. I have decided to name them 'Lady Lovely' and 'Starman'.

It took great efforts on Dad's part to drag me back into breakfast and soon I knew why he was so keen. He handed me a case with a red bow tied on the handle, and inside was a second-hand saxophone in great, great condition! I can't believe that I'll finally be playing an instrument I love, and I can already sight-read music thanks to my years of scratching away on a violin. I've decided that, although Mum and Dad would pay for lessons, I want to pay for them myself with the money I earned on the film.

Ro is using her wages (plus all her Christmas money since she was born, practically) to buy a second-hand film camera because she has decided that she wants to be a director. She has asked me and Stephen to write a script for a fifteen-minute short which we're going to make in three weeks time. I told her we could have it ready in two, but she said three so that Alex will have flown out and won't expect to star in it – that honour goes to Paul, of course. The whole thing could be amazing or amazingly disastrous, but I don't really mind as I know we'll have loads of fun. We invited Nick to scout out some locations for us, but he's decided that he just wants to hang out in town for the rest of the summer so we've given that job to Gussy who is proving remarkably (very remarkably) good at it.

The wrap party is tonight and I'm beside myself with excitement, especially as I adore the outfit I bought during the Granger Girls' shopping trip. Lorna had decided she might or might not dance with Alex (if you can call that a decision) and Alice is concerned that her dress is too patterned and it might ruin her entire night. Sophie has phoned ten times in the last two hours.

The whole gang of us are meeting at The Grange at lunchtime to help prepare the party. I'm so glad they decided to have it in the ballroom, Stephen is really glad that they'll have pancakes, and Lorna and Alice are *thrilled* that my dad was able to talk their folks into letting them be at the party as they initially felt it must just be for the adults working on the film.

Stephen just called and I told him that I *love* my present of the 'Teach Yourself Chinese' course, and the new fountain pen is just *perfect*. While we were talking about this and that I told him that when you do the computer love-compatibility test, 'Lemony and Stephen' comes out at 95 per cent. He said not to worry, he'll soon sort out that last troublesome 5 per cent.

Oh yes! The game of life is a good one.